The Flight
of The Starling

A Fairy Tale

Ella Arrow

Dedication

To my grandparents, Marguerite and Charles, who would always read me books, and Della, whose life was an adventure.

Table of Contents

Part One
In which We Meet a Beautiful Princess with an
Interest In Fairies

Once upon a time, there lived a beautiful princess with the most amazing collection of magical artifacts ever assembled this side of Merlin's boot closet (which historians have never been able to locate and therefore never catalog, but we can assume some pretty terrific magical thingamajigs were in it, so I'm sure you get what I mean).

This princess (whose name, if you want to know, was Lily) had long flowing locks of chestnut hair, and eyes that were, depending on her mood and the weather outside, sometimes green, sometimes brown, and, occasionally, golden. They were always fiery. Her eyebrows seemed always to be asking a question, and her lips looked like they knew the answer. Her nose, I'm afraid, was remarkably dull, but overall the people of her kingdom of Starling found her "radiant" and "stunning – a royal gem!" (Sir Scandalot of the *Knightly Times*).

Princess Lily had a magical mirror with one side that showed you the person you always hoped you might be, and the other showed your inner, true, undeniable self. Princess Lily liked to use this device to look under her bed. Mostly she saw dust bunnies munching around, and one or two home gnomes who must not have liked themselves much, based on what the mirror showed her.

She had a magical key ring that always came when you called it, only it happened to have a name that was hard to pronounce (try to say "ghoti" while sneezing). If Princess Lily didn't get the inflection just right, the key ring's feelings were hurt, and it would sulk for days and not come out. She'd given up locking her lavatory, rather than risk never seeing daylight again.

Princess Lily had scads and scores of these kinds of magical artifacts. Little dolls that danced the tarantella. Crystals that sang, only slightly off-key, when the sun shone on them. A hat that always made your hair look better, instead of worse. They coated the shelves in her bed chamber. They dripped off the end tables onto the floor. They made sweeping under the bed nearly impossible, much to the delight of the dust bunnies.

On the day of the Grand Duke's son's bris, Princess Lily and her friend, Alistrina, were out in the kitchen garden using magical artifacts to hunt for fairies. The princess knew fairies existed, but she'd never personally seen one, the way you know grizzly bears are real but haven't run into any on your way to the pickle emporium. The Grand Duke was rumored to keep fairy servants, and since baby-related ceremonies are favorable times to have Little Folk around, he might have brought them to Castle Starling. Princess Lily hoped so, anyway.

"Anything yet?" Princess Lily asked her friend.

"I'm afraid not." Alistrina, a blonde, solid girl whose only true beauty was the perfect orderliness of her teeth, waved her hand around in slow circles in front of her. She turned toward different parts of the late-spring garden, the green vines climbing trellises, neat rows of vegetables, and sunshine filtering through the fruit trees near the sandstone courtyard wall. "Not a flicker on this Fairy Ring." The large gem in the Ring she wore – magicked to change color in the presence of fairy folk – was a soft and resolute blue. "What about you, see anything special?"

Princess Lily adjusted the large pink spectacles she wore over her amazing eyes. "Well, that goat over there should really be chased out of the turnip patch." She pointed to a male gardener pulling turnips up by the root. He sat back and stroked his rather pointy beard, and laughed. Lily waved a hand at him and said, "Shoo!"

Alistrina rolled her eyes, deciding not to explain this to the princess, who began collecting magical artifacts because of her obsession with fairies. In the Enlightened Kingdoms, an average family might have two or three treasured magical items, passed down as precious heirlooms, and royalty like the Starlings had a few dozen amusing trinkets, but still needed servants to sweep and cook and garden in a most un-magical manner. "Perhaps the Rose-Colored Glasses aren't working," suggested Alistrina. "Shouldn't they be showing the magical creatures around you, not goats?"

"They're supposed to see through magical enchantments, so if a fairy is disguised behind a glamour, I should be able to see it," said the princess. "Come on, there's nothing out here. Let's try the kitchen."

Cooks were pulling copper pots off racks, chopping vegetables and lamb on different ends of the chopping blocks in the castle's large kitchen, and otherwise stirring, baking, or bustling around to make the feast.

"I don't understand why your father doesn't just get you a fairy. Can't the king get you anything you want?" Alistrina nicked a pastry from a basket and shared a smile with the baker.

Alistrina was from the neighboring realm of Lualdath, so the ways of Starling and King William were foreign to her. "My father banned fairies from the kingdom," explained Princess Lily, leaning back against the wooden counter. "When my father was a prince, my grandfather tried to give him a fairy companion, but granddad didn't know much about fairies. He ended up getting a changeling, which was just a boy with slightly pointy ears. My dad got along with 'Fred the fairy' for a while, but when he started refusing to eat his special diet of green leaves and sunshine, and wanted to share the prince's human food, people figured it out. My father always says this fascination with fairies is nonsense liable to lead to disappointment and a smaller share of cake. When he became king, he fired all the fairy servants. Only really special guests like the Grand Duke are even allowed to bring them in, and only if my father doesn't have to feed them."

"But you were telling me about home gnomes who stole your keys. Don't they count?"

"Other fae-kind are still allowed. Ever since last fall's

Curdled Custard Fiasco, I've suspected trolls of haunting the castle. But fairies aren't welcome, and it's been so many years, now they mostly stay away."

"Not that it keeps her highness from looking for them," piped in a baker, vigorously kneading dough nearby. "We all know what you're looking for, highness, with them rosy specs." The large woman nodded her head knowingly.

"I've never actually seen a fairy," Lily finished wistfully.

Many girls love stories about pixies, nixies, and sprites, but Lily's obsession went beyond the typical, in spite of, and perhaps because, her father was the one who had pushed them out of her reach. Princess Lily thought of fairies the way some girls think of "bad boys." She knew very well that they could be mischievous, sly, and selfish, but they were also dashing, mysterious, forbidden, and incredibly romantic. If a fairy had shown up at Castle Starling wearing a motorcycle jacket and a disrespect for authority, you can be sure Princess Lily would have been head over heels before he spoke a word with his pouty, mutinous mouth.

Alistrina had more ordinary interests for a teenage girl. "How long are we going to keep looking? I saw the courtiers as they came in, and some of them were unbelievably cute. I don't want to miss our chance to ... bump into them." Alistrina raised her eyebrows, implying many possibilities.

The princess resettled the Glasses on her nose. "We haven't even finished *this* room yet. We'll make it in time it to the feast after the ceremony."

Alistrina sighed. "Alright but if the boy with the blue leaf doublet is talking to some other maiden by the time we get there, I may never forgive you."

The search of the kitchen turned up bupkus – which is to say no fairies – as did the scullery, the servants' quarters, the Tower Of The Moon and the one Of The Sun. Several times Alistrina reminded Princess Lily of her promise to get to the party. The princess reminded Alistrina whose castle she was in, then, feeling a twinge of remorse, repeated her promise that they could go soon.

Finally in the guest wing, they began to get results with their fairy detecting gear. Lily knew the bedspread on the large four-poster bed to be green, but it looked an awful mustard color with her pink Glasses. The person lodging in this room must've had some kind of pet, for a small iron cage lay on the floor in one corner, with a soft pillow inside and two small dishes for food and water.

"The Fairy Ring is flickering! I think it's changing color," Alistrina said. "Oh, good goblins, it was but only for a second."

"Don't swear, it's un-lady-like," shushed Princess Lily.

"And sneaking into guest's rooms isn't?"

Lily hesitated. It *wasn't* proper to sneak into people's rooms, even in her own castle, but she couldn't think of a better chance to see a fairy in person, something she had yearned for all her life. She knew better than to ask straight out about the Grand Duke's fairies – her father would surely make her sit through the hours-long "fairy nonsense" lecture again.

Finally she said, a high justifying tone slipping into her voice, "It's not as if we're snooping for people's secrets. We're only looking for fairies."

Alistrina laughed. "It's never 'only' with you, highness. Not when it's anything to do with fairies."

Princess Lily looked around the guest room with her Rose-Colored Glasses. Everything in the room looked ordinary, though pinkish. "Maybe we should stop now and just go to the par–"

She stopped abruptly, and pointed under a small table near the open door.

"Over there!" the princess whispered. "I see this faint trail of glitter. Try the Ring."

Alistrina held her hand up where Lily pointed, as both girls took a silent step closer.

"I think it's ... yes ... it's changing to green." They looked at the Ring as its neutral blue faded and transformed slowly to a swirling green, that meant a fairy had at long last been found.

They squealed in excitement and clasped each other's hands. When they looked back at the Ring, the green was fading back to blue again. "What's happening?" asked Alistrina.

The trail of glitter led from the original spot through the open door. "It's on the run," said Lily. "Quick!"

They ran out into the hallway which was lined with floor-to-ceiling tapestries. Quickly they figured out the fairy was heading in the direction of the Second Most Grand Hall. Though they couldn't see the creature itself, they saw where it rippled the thick tapestries as it ran. The Fairy Ring kept detecting, flashing various colors as they chased it. The glittery shine the princess could see was strongest at the head of the trail, fading behind the fairy like the tail of a comet.

It was incredibly fast. Even as the girls ran down the hallway, the fairy was several yards ahead of them and they barely gained on it. Before they could get within a yard of it, they were all running into the Second Most Grand Hall and the crowded court.

The hall was a series of white plaster arches which intersected in three connected domes high overhead, with a delicate sandy yellow on the rounded walls in between. A plinth at the base of each arch held a potted ivy plant, which climbed and clung to the walls as the only decoration. Right then the hall was standing room only, with a rabbi, the duke's family, and the king and queen on a little dais in front of a few hundred courtiers. The guest of honor was fussing and wondering when someone would change his diaper.

The princess and her friend looked anxiously over the heads of the throng, along the floor between noble knees, and then they began weaving through the crowd.

"A wing, I saw a wing! Just there, over that man's shoulder!" Lily pointed.

"Yes, there's green in that direction! Get closer!"

Anxious not to lose it, the maidens moved quickly, brushing and bumping past people to reach a short man with the most beautiful head of hair the princess had ever seen. On one shoulder of his gold jacket, peeking out from behind his collar, was a slender shimmering wing with purple tracings and an iridescent shine.

Behind her Glasses the princess's eyes blinked from brown to green as a thrill swept through her chest. Lily pointed with her naked finger. Alistrina pointed with her ring finger. They nodded, and stepped toward the man.

He wasn't much taller than Princess Lily. Turning toward Lily, he gave them a smile in silent greeting, which turned a little confused with an uplift of his brow, then downright alarmed as the brow flipped a U-ey when he realized their intense gaze was targeting him. He shifted his weight nervously from one foot to the other, and took a step backward.

The princess stared intently at his shoulder. Alistrina strained on tiptoe a little as the shoulder in question was turned away from her. As they approached, the Fairy Ring flickered green/ blue/green/red/blue, and the Rose-Colored Glasses showed the gossamer wing slip out of sight around the man's tall collar.

Princess Lily circled around to see the fairy. The small, glittering winged person looked up at her with knowing black eyes. By this point the little man was so perplexed and disquieted that when she reached for the fairy, he could do nothing but throw up his hands and emit a little shriek of terror.

Fortunately for our princess, at that same moment the ceremony concluded and everyone in the crowd was throwing up their hands and cheering. With the man's sudden movement, the dainty creature clutched at his jacket with its tiny fingers, then fell. The man's arm bumped Lily and her Glasses flew off, her eyes flashing bright green. The fairy fell into her waiting hands as Lily held her breath in elation and wonder at her first real fairy encounter.

But what landed in her hands, and what she saw with her unmagical, fiery eyes, wasn't a fairy at all. It was long, furry, and weasel-like, with small rounded ears, a pointy pleasant face, short legs and a skinny tail. The animal was soft and white and looked up at her with knowing black eyes.

"Oh your highness, you gave me such a fright," said the little man. Without the Glasses, Lily could see his coat was a light brown, not cloth-of-gold at all. His hair was as far from beautiful as a grown man can wear: streaks of greasy hair combed over a freckled bald spot.

"If only I had known your highness was interested in ferrets, I would have gladly shown you Stanley when the bris was over. But there, I see he likes you."

"Stanley?" said Alistrina, in wonderment, finally getting a look at the creature.

"Ferret?" squeaked Princess Lily in disbelief. She looked down to see Stanley the Ferret chewing experimentally on the lace of her cuff, then give it up for a bad job and climb inside her wide bell sleeve. His tiny claws dug into the flesh of her arm.

She tried to grab him inside the sleeve without success, and Alistrina touched the outside of the dress to guide him out. Her Ring pulsed a most excited shade of green where her hand lay over the ferret. She and the princess locked eyes.

"Alistrina, are you absolutely sure that's a Fairy Ring?" Her voice dropped to a dead-serious tone, or at least as serious as she could manage while trying to wrestle the ferret out of her dress.

"My maid **said** it was when she opened my birthday gifts and read me the cards." Alistrina's face contorted in remorse and confusion. "I suppose it's **possible** I didn't hear her right...."

"Are these yours, my dear?" The combed-over man handed the pink spectacles back to Princess Lily. "My brother has a pair of those. Magic shows you what you want to see most in the world. He married the ugliest girl I ever seen in my life, and lived happily with her these 20 years.

"And I see you've got a Ferret Ring!" He amiably brought up his hand to show Alistrina a ring the exact copy of her own. "No wonder you were both so keen on meeting Stanley. I never take mine off when I travel with him, makes no end of difference when trying to find him behind the couch cushions."

Lily took one last hopeful jab for the day at her lifelong wish. "I don't suppose you know whether the Grand Duke brought his fairy servants to the castle, do you?"

"No, his manservant was complaining to my manservant that he had ever so much more work because they left the fairies at home. Wouldn't do to upset the king when he's your host," the ferret owner said with a smile.

By now Stanley had emerged from Lily's sleeve onto her collarbone, where he was licking her neck and earlobe. It was a warm, cuddly sort of a thing, and it tickled. Lily was no longer startled by the ferret, and despite her disappointment over her failed fairy hunt, she couldn't help laughing.

Part Two
In which Princess Lily Discovers a Magical Book

After her unintentionally successful ferret-hunt, Princess Lily began to wonder if her experiments with magical artifacts were going wrong for a reason. Perhaps she needed something that would educate her, enlighten her, instead of merely attempt to locate fairies for her. Truth through wisdom, rather than blind muddling.

"None of my magical artifacts work like they should," she complained to her mother, the queen. "The mistakes with the Rose-Colored Glasses and Ferret Ring have made me see my collection in a new light. I see so many flaws I never saw before. Why can't I find a really useful magical artifact? One that will teach me real facts about fairies instead of just tales?"

"Or even something to take your mind off fairies," suggested the queen, frowning slightly. "It would certainly make your father's mind easier. Why don't you get some new magical toys? You could find better ones, with stronger magic and fewer flaws, than what you already have. I'll have your lady, Martha, invite all the magical merchants up to the castle tomorrow for you. Find something to expand your horizons beyond this useless quest for fairies."

"What a splendid idea, Mum," she said. "Yes, send them to set up in the Second Most Grand Hall, and I'll go shopping like it was a bazaar!" With a peck on queen-mum's cheek, she left the room smiling.

The next day, all the magical merchants had lined the Second Most Grand Hall with colorful booths. The royal minstrels (Sir Robin's Merry Men and One Woman) set up at the far end of the hall to provide ambiance. The lords and ladies of the court, and one or two kitchen wenches who had been saving up, also came to shop at the magical bazaar.

So many different items were available, in a wide range of prices – from flying carpets for 5,000 gold pieces, to smart phones for 200 gold, to sweet spoons that meant you'd never over-sugar your oatmeal again for only 5 gold. Lily and her lady-in-waiting perused them all.

By the time they'd gone from one end of the Second Most Grand Hall to the other, Lily was beginning to feel disheartened. She hadn't found anything that called to her, anything that would help her in her fairy quest or even discover more about the world. Martha tried to keep Princess Lily's spirits up, getting worried as Lily's eyes turned darker and darker shades of brown.

"Come, your highness, do let's look at those magic rings again. I still say the Ring of Green Dragon's Dreams could be the one." Lily let herself be pulled along by Martha's insistent tug at her wrist.

The Ring of Green Dragon's Dreams was just as boring as before. *Doesn't anyone sell magical artifacts that let one look beyond oneself?* thought Lily. They were all so selfish: a ring that let you spy on a dragon's dreams, or a sweater that let you disguise yourself, or a bracelet that made you unbeatable at bowling. As she tilted her head in despair, her gaze fell on a booth she hadn't noticed before. Considerably more shabby than the others, a moth-eaten blanket covered a low table, on which a very few books were laid out. Behind the table sat an old woman in a rocking chair with a shawl over her shoulders. She was whistling a marvelous little tune that reminded Lily of a swollen brook in springtime.

Since Martha seemed occupied with the rings, Lily stepped over to the booth. A small, handwritten sign lay flat on the table:

> *Heddy Winchester*
> *Purveyor of Fine Words*
> *and Other Verbal Necessities*
> *Punctuation Free with Every Purchase*

The old woman looked up in time to see Lily smiling. She

was short, roundish, and lumpy as a mountain of mashed potatoes. Her vaguely blue shawl was threadbare, as if she wore it out of habit and not for warmth. Her straggling hair was grey, silver, and black. But her eyes were a lively pale green and when she returned Lily's smile, the princess felt fond of her immediately.

"So you're a 'purveyor of fine words.' What do you sell... exactly?" Princess Lily asked as kindly as she knew how.

"Well," said Heddy, "what do you need?"

After a short, bewildered silence, she went on. "I sell That Word You Were Thinking Of, for starters. Also got Sarcasm Sensors, and some Snappy Comebacks. Very handy, those are. Got a couple of Joke Bombs, one or two Argument Edge Cards." Here Heddy leaned in conspiratorially near the princess. "I also got a vial of Silver Tongue Syrup. Very rare, that is. One drop and you'd charm the pants off of any man around. Not, that is to say, that your 'ighness needs any help with such matters."

Lily shook her lovely head. "No, I wouldn't want to charm someone using magic. Don't you have anything ... insightful?"

"Wait." Heddy held up a wrinkled finger. "I've got it. You'll be wanting the Book of Enlightenment. Hang on." Heddy doubled over to poke in a sack below the table. After some moments of rummaging and grumbling, including a few "Huh?"s, an "Ew," and finally an "Aha," Heddy produced an enormous tome and set it on the table with a heavy thud.

The table was so low that the princess could not get close enough to the Book when standing up. She looked one direction, then the other, to be sure no one was watching, then she knelt.

"The Book of Enlightenment," she murmured, running her hand over the worn and battered cover. The Book was bound in thick black leather, with little slats of wood going cross-wise as if for reinforcement, and tiny iron nails in the binding. In the center was an icon of a large eye with a lightning bolt in its pupil.

"What does it do?" Lily asked.

"It tells you what you need to know," answered Heddy, opening the Book. "Sometimes it'll just tell you things, if they're so urgent they can't wait for you to sit down and read. Other times, you'll need to browse for information, or you can go to the index and ask a question."

Heddy flipped to the back of the Book to a section that said "Index" in fancy script across the top of a page. It showed nothing but a few letters of the alphabet in such a large size they seemed to be waiting for attention. "Now, think of something you want to know, and say your question to the Book's index. Then the Book will go to the right page and tell you what you need to know."

Lily leaned in a little and said, "Tell me about the Book of Enlightenment." Words appeared under the large letter "B": "Book of Enlightenment, page xii." Then the pages started to flip on their own, causing a little breeze that made Lily lean back as it fluttered her dark brown hair and made her blink. Finally it stopped near the front of the Book, where a heading read, "Welcome to the Book of Enlightenment."

> The Book of Enlightenment was first created by the great wizard Melvin Marleybone in the Age of Groovy Spells and Potions. He gave it to the Fifth Earl of Purrcell in the kingdom of Felination. The Earl enjoyed use of the Book for many years until he inexplicably threw it out his bedroom window one night, exclaiming, "You could have told me that YESTERDAY!"

"Isn't there anything about what the book does, and not just its history?" Lily asked Heddy.

Before Heddy could answer, the Book flipped a single page, and the beginning of a paragraph glowed and seemed to hover above the surface of the page.

> The Book is full of Useful Information about geographic regions, diverse zoologics, a few celebrities and other nefarious persons, plants (edible, poisonous, and edible but extremely unpleasant to taste), dragons, elves, gnomes, fairies, wandering tribes, historical castles, labyrinths of the Enlightened Kingdoms, yoga, aromatherapy, auras, oracles, the secret language of cats, how to win at Mah

Jong without cheating, and just about any other subject the reader can imagine.

The Book gets its information by tapping into the collective unconscious of the universe, which is a force that binds people everywhere together with an invisible, psychic link. The Book's connection to the collective unconscious, its conduit if you will, is the mind of the reader, so the contents are affected by the opinions and beliefs of the reader, and those people in the nearest vicinity. If any information read here is inaccurate, it is because the reader and her closest society has an incorrect perception about the subject. Because of this, the Book is slightly different for every reader. Overall the content is relatively consistent, however.

This also means that the Book will change as the reader changes and learns. It can essentially 'remember' lessons and information the reader has encountered. The Book of Enlightenment can guide you and grow with you.™

"Yes, but how do you tell me what I need to know, like Heddy said?" asked Lily, speaking now directly to the Book. Another paragraph glowed.

The Book can be used as a reference guide on a particular topic of interest. Most readers prefer a more active approach. When confronted with a situation in her adventures which requires immediate information, the reader may ask the Book, "What's the magic word to call off an attack troll?" The Book gives a brief answer to such a specific question ("spatula"). When asking general questions, the Book gives you essential or important information on the topic first, and you may ask more specific questions as you go.

The Book also features the Emergency Alert System. If the Book senses through the collective unconscious that its reader needs to know something important, the Book automatically presents this information without being asked.

"Read enough, dearie?" Heddy broke in. "Cuz I hate to be

rude, but I've to ask, are you by any chance the Princess Lily?"

Lily raised her head importantly, as much as she could while kneeling with the old lady hunching over her. "Yes, I am Princess Lily."

"Oh, good!" Heddy clapped her hands. "Because I just remembered, I read in there this morning that you're the one I was goin' to sell it to. I'd hate to sell it to somebody else when it's meant to be yours. A'course, no one else's even been to my booth, so I s'pose it turned out right either way."

"What do you mean, you read that I would buy it?" asked Lily suspiciously. "You're not trying to pull a fast one on me, are you?"

"Oh dear, no," said Heddy through her chuckles. "I'm too old to do much of anything fast. No, it's in the Book, see." She turned back to the Introduction and said, "History of ownership, uh, recent additions."

Far down on the right-hand page, at what appeared to be the end of a section, the following sentences glowed and floated off the page:

> *In the 27th year of the reign of King William Henry Starling the 5th, the king's only daughter, Princess Lily Rose Violet Starling, acquired the Book from a wisewoman, Heddy Winchester (purveyor of Fine Words and Other Verbal Necessities), to whom it had belonged for 368 years. Shortly after purchasing the Book, the princess began a journey of self-discovery that caused*

"It stops." Lily anxiously turned the page over, but it only had the heading of a new section, "Curing What Ails You: Potions, Brews, and Love Philters from the Enlightened Kingdoms."

"Where's the rest of the sentence?" asked Lily in bewilderment. This time the Book did not answer: no pages turned, no words floated, no new text appeared.

"It doesn't know everything, dearie. It only knows what the universe knows, which is a little ways into the future, but it can't predict very much. Why, those sentences weren't there yesterday, but two hours ago when I looked it up, there your name was. 'Oh,' I says to myself, 'I guess I'm selling this today.'" Heddy shrugged her sloped shoulders under her shawl.

Lily twitched her nose in contemplation, still not sure it wasn't a trick. But after all, the Book *was* the only magical artifact that might offer more than trivial interest, and it did seem capable of teaching her things she needed to know.

"Alright, how much do you want for it?" she said, standing up.

"One thousand gold pieces, an' it please you," Heddy answered with a slight bow.

Lily stood up a little taller, put her shoulders back, and stuck out her chin just a little. She tried her best to look serious and royal, and said, "Seven hundred fifty."

Heddy chuckled, her smile crinkling her entire face up to her eyes. "That's good, Lady. Never take anyone's first offer! Now that Book's very rare and not worth a haypenny less than nine 'undred, for a clever lass like you."

Lily snapped her fingers and gave instructions to the nearest castle servant, who soon returned dragging a large leather bag clearly too heavy to lift. With a mutter and a faint scowl, he got on his knees, opened the bag, and began counting out gold coins in little stacks on Heddy's table. "Five, ten, fifteen...."

As Lily reached down for the Book, the old lady suddenly grabbed her by the wrist. Lily was startled that she would dare lay a hand on her so rudely.

"I would ask that your highness be careful." Heddy leaned in very closely as she pulled the princess closer. Lily stared as Heddy slowly licked her lips, and then whispered so very faintly that she wasn't quite sure of what she heard: "A little knowledge is a dangerous thing." The withered wet lips tugged into a small, taut smirk. Then Heddy released her and stood back with the same placid, good-natured smile on her unremarkable face.

Heddy hummed like nothing had happened, like the facade of the gentle old woman had never been broken. Lily didn't know what to say. *She's a silly old woman, and you're an intelligent and beautiful princess*, she thought. *Just laugh about it. It's nothing.*

But what could she mean by such nothing?

Heddy began whistling her marvelous tune again and started to pack up her booth.

"You take care, dearie," she said, only a hint of that awful menacing smirk in her smile. She bent to continue packing, paying no more attention to the princess.

Apparently dismissed, the stunned princess picked up her Book and clutched it to her chest. It wasn't nearly as heavy as it looked. She turned away from the booth as Martha came up to her, brandishing a new ring. Straining not to look back, to examine Heddy further, Princess Lily led the way out of the hall.

Part Three
In which Princess Lily Meets a Fairy or Two

A great change took over the land after the day Lily bought the Book of Enlightenment. It started at the castle. As you know, the prosperity, happiness, and general state of dental hygiene in any kingdom worth its salt is largely dependent upon the princess. In particular, said princess's ability to laugh, smile, and make the stars shine with her ethereal glow.

I've already told you how lovely Princess Lily was, but since acquiring the Book, she had really begun to shine. She was so shiny, in fact, that all the treasures of the palace – the crown jewels, the polished mahogany thrones, the silver ewers, the rings on the queen's fingers and toes, even the bald head of Sir Robin the minstrel – everything seemed dull and dusky when she walked into the room.

Lily read night and day. Her embroidery fell by the wayside. Her riding instructor was forced to take up a hobby. She barely made an appearance at court on presentation day. The only thing she really took time out for was her archery, which she thoroughly enjoyed for the precision involved and the exercise that kept her arms strong.

No more wild magical experiments. No more sighs over their inevitable failures. Imagine it – *her eyes always stayed green!* She was a woman transformed, and her kingdom was transformed with her.

"Our daughter has really come into her own of late," said King William to his Queen Elizabeth one day. "Why, she can discourse on everything from the history of home gnomes to the proper stance for winning at croquet. Ain't she clever!"

"I wish she'd *do* some of the things she's been reading about. She's always got her nose in that book, although one is less likely to notice how dull her nose is, then." The queen polished her emerald ring to elicit more shine.

"At last she has found a grown-up hobby instead of this childish obsession with fairy folk. I couldn't be prouder."

"Well, I'm glad you're happy, but her interest in fairies never hurt anybody," said the queen.

The king ignored this last remark, thinking he was harmed by a large helping of annoyance over it. He went straight on to his point. "Well, I've thought of something that will make her take an interest in things not in books. I do believe the time be right for getting her a suitable husband."

"The time *is* right," muttered the queen, squinting into her gem.

"I mean, look at how happy and prosperous the kingdom is these days. The milkmaids sing when they get up before dawn, when no one in their right mind would be happy to be out of bed, and their cows are putting out twice the milk the castle needs. Everywhere flowers are blooming, crop yields are increasing. It always seems to rain only at night now, so that all is green but nobody has to get wet."

"And no more mood-changing eyes," the queen put in.

"Exactly," said the king. "Green and golden everywhere, and no more brown. I bet we can get her a right smart catch if we put out the word for suitable suitors."

As it turned out, the king's Word didn't get any farther than the Rose Vine Courtyard of Castle Starling, because another Word had already decided to take a trip up and down the countryside. That very afternoon, the first of many suitors rode into the Rose Vine Courtyard, having heard the other word about Lily's beauty and the kingdom's wealth. Before the day was out, the stables held more than two dozen white horses, making a nightmare for the grooms to tell one from another.

Almost the same could be said of the suitors. Many were princes from distant lands, such as Lualdath to the south, Sweethaven to the east, and Cloudland to the north by northwest. There were also some dukes, an earl, and one king from a tiny country called Rhode Island.

All had brought gifts to impress the princess and her parents, but the gifts showed the lack of cleverness in the suitors: twenty had brought bouquets of lilies, roses, and violets, for each of the princess's names. One, slightly better, than the rest, had brought live plants.

While the white horses were being stabled, the princes were shown into the Absolutely Most Grand Hall to be presented to king and queen, and these many flower arrangements were placed on every available end table in the castle, Princess Lily was up in the Tower of Shining Stars, reading the Book, none the wiser to the adventures in courting awaiting her at court.

She had just finished a chapter on goblins, and their love of a nice flaky pastry, so she turned to the section called Daily Confirmations. This part of the Book would give you little glimpses into your future.

"Book," said Lily, "what's the weather going to be like today?"

The heading "Weather" glowed.

> *Today will begin sunny and blue, with a positive outlook. Just after sunset, a deep, Dickensian fog will roll in and a little while later, it will roll out again, taking a number of important things with it.*

"Oh," said Lily in some startlement. "Will it rain again tonight?" Rain was common at night, but not fog.

> *Rain expected tonight and tomorrow and into Tuesday-week.*

Knowing the Book often mixed metaphors with forecasting, she asked, "What will roll in and out with the fog?"

"*Royalty,*" said the Book.

She was just about to ask whether this involved her directly when she was distracted by a commotion at the windowsill near where she sat.

"Ssssshht!" was actually the first sound she heard. Then, a high voice whispered, "I fink that must be her."

"Sh!" Clearly there were two voices. But where were they? The courtyard was nine stories below; no sound could have wafted up from there no matter how ambitious the breeze. Lily turned in her seat toward the window, looking about.

The tapestry that normally covered the window – pulled back now to let in more light by which to read – fluttered and moved at the far corner of the window.

"She'll hear you, you dimwit," said the shushing voice.

"Naw, she don't 'ear me. She's lookin' out ta window."

At this, Lily let the Book slip down onto her chair. She watched the rustling curtain out of the corner of her eye. She couldn't help noticing a lot of white horses in the courtyard.

"Caw, she is a fancy one, then, prettier than her legend, even," said the second voice in a slight accent. "He 'ad nuffing to worry about."

Who had nothing to worry about? thought Lily. *They're not trolls, that's for sure.* Trolls hated small rooms and poetical names, so the Tower of Shining Stars was a troll-free zone.

Still looking out the window, Lily slowly stood up and casually inched her way toward the sill.

"Yeh, she is a beauty," agreed the shusher. "Wos sat book, though? Ya don't fink she's some kinda book-reading ninny? She'll go cross-eyed and he'll throw her in an oubliette, fer sure."

Lily shivered at the thought of an oubliette. She had learned the word when reading about dungeons: a deep pit into which someone was thrown and forgotten. She reached the sill and laid her hands gently upon it. She could just make out the forms of two tiny people standing on the other end of the sill, in the shadow of the tapestry.

Couldn't be home gnomes, thought Lily. Home gnome language is a series of ticks, groans, wheezes, and thumps meant to sound like ordinary household noises. However strange this dialect was, it was certainly Lily's own language.

"He wouldn't throw her in the oubliette," argued the

second voice. "Not if she was his queen. Naw, that wouldn't do. He'd prolly just lock her in a tower."

The figures gesticulated in their argument, moving in and out of the shadow, making the sunlight glint off the wings that rose from their shoulders.

Fairies!

Lily sucked in her breath. Real fairies! In her reading room! She let the breath out slowly, with great care, to keep control of her excitement. She wanted to jump and shout, to call the fairies out of their hiding place, to ask them what they were doing in her room, how did they take their coffee, what did they do for fun on a Saturday night?

Wait, she thought, as she took another deep breath to regain her slipping composure. *What are they doing in my room, whispering from a dark corner?*

Lily decided to catch them by surprise. She leaned forward very slowly, moving toward the tapestry's pull. She glanced at them quickly now and again so they would still think she hadn't noticed them.

"Yer prolly right. But all this is moot if he doesn't win her. A scoundrel like 'im, I'd be surprised if the king didn't see right through him."

Lily's hand was an inch away from the silken rope that held the tapestry. *Please don't fly away before I really get to see you!*

"I don't see how he's goin' to tell one o' dese blokes from another ta pick a husband, he's so daft."

"My father is not daft!"

Quick as a titmouse, Lily's hand grabbed the cord and snapped it away from the fastening. The tapestry unfurled with a heavy *whoosh* and the two interlopers waved their arms as they lost their balance and fell to the floor, unfurling their wings to avoid disaster at the last moment.

The curtain fell, completely covering the window. The little folk were trapped. With only candlelight in the room, Lily squinted at them, leaning forward as her dark tresses flowed before her.

"You **are** fairies!" she shouted, as if she hadn't really believed it until she saw them. Clearly one was a boy, in short pants similar to lederhosen (which is a quaint if silly-looking style of German shorts with suspenders) and a light green tunic. His hair was a bit mossy and his wings looked a lot like the first leaves of an apple tree in spring. The girl was taller, wearing scrappy blue overalls with a lavender shirt that almost clashed with her bright blue hair and blue and white moth-like wings.

"Who – who are you," she stammered, "and what are you doing in my room?" Lily's heart spun and fluttered and did jumping jacks at the sight of the creatures she had wanted to meet since she was a little girl.

The boy fairy stood on the floor, hunched forward, apparently forgetting that he could fly. He had a big, daft, toothy grin plastered on his face and his eyes twitched rapidly from side to side, as if somehow his stupid smile would be sufficient camouflage. The girl fairy, much more practical-minded, flew up to the side of the tapestry and maniacally tugged, trying to move it away from the wall and make her escape. Luckily it was a very heavily embroidered thing, with many woolen goat-men prancing after many maidens. The goats simply overpowered the fairy.

"You may as well give it up," Lily put her hands on her hips, "and just tell me who you are."

The girl fairy gave one more fruitless tug on the fabric for good measure, bracing her feet against the stone wall, then turned around to face the princess. She floated down and kicked the other fairy soundly in the buttocks, saying simply, "Stop that. She can see you."

Straightening up, the boy looked sheepish, and stopped grinning.

"I am Marzipan," said the girl, "and this is Beloit. We were sent by the prince of Sweethaven ta see if you really are as beau'iful as he was told, since he's come here to ask for yer hand in marriage."

"What do you mean, he's asked to marry me? Is he here

now? How can I marry someone I don't know?" Lily's questions rolled out of her mouth one on top of the other.

Marzipan rolled her dark purple eyes and crossed her arms. With exasperated patience, she held out one finger for each question she answered. "He's 'ere to ask ta marry you, by asking your dad, ya know, the king." She held a second finger up. "A'course he's 'ere now because we're his servants and he brought us t' yer castle." A third finger. "He wants ta marry ya because ye're famously beau'iful and now yer father's kingdom is very rich." Marzipan crossed her arms again and raised her bright blue eyebrows to inquire if this was sufficient answer.

"Well, I . . . but . . ." Lily sputtered for a moment. *That must explain the white horses,* she thought. *Should I offer them something to drink? To eat? I could call a servant. No, they insulted my father and talked of oubliettes. I must find out what they're about.*

She took a deep breath once more to restrain her curiosity and jubilation, so she could attempt to act sensibly. "What sort of man is this prince, your master? It's **awfully** improper for him to send spies."

"Actually I'd be surprised if we was the only ones," Beloit spoke for the first time. He seemed to remember the princess suddenly, and out came the cheeky smile again.

"Improper is the least of it," said Marzipan. "Prince Alexander is a dirty pig of a man, totally spoilt, **disgusting** manners" – Marzipan spat the word – "right beastly treatment of his servants, and anyone who isn't his rank or higher." She cocked her head at Princess Lily, and said, "Your royal highness," with exaggerated reverence, slowly leaning into a sloppy mockery of a courtly bow.

"How do I know you're telling the truth?" Lily began to pace through the chamber, hands clasped behind her back in a formal interrogation pose she had seen her father use. "Maybe you weren't sent by Prince Alexander at all. Maybe you were sent by one of his rivals."

At this Beloit rolled his eyes skyward, er, ceilingward, and let out a grand sigh. "Yeah, 'cuz there's a whole load o' blokes out there wot are more sneaky than our sneaky rascal of a master. And we've come up here ta help **them** out. Sure. Ye're onto us." Beloit began some pacing of his own, gesturing wildly. "Some other nasty royal twit has sent us all the way up here, threat'ning us if we don't get caught whisperin' about another prince behind a heavy curtain!

"Do you," he said slowly, "have any idear. How hard, and how tiring, and how bloody long. It took. Fer me and my sister t' fly all the way up here? Crikey, I've only got a 5-inch wingspan, and Marzi's ain't much more than that. This castle has twelve-foot ceilings, and wiv quarried stone of this size, that makes the stories a good 15 ta 18 feet high, and when you take into account wind velocity –"

"It's alright. I believe you," Lily jumped in, a faint smile brightening up her face as she looked at the beautiful little fairies. "I guess you must be telling the truth. And you say your master is a bad man?"

Marzipan looked at the floor a moment, then directly into Lily's eyes. The fairy looked sad, which is not something Lily expected to see in such a light and frivolous-looking creature. "He threatened ta cut our wings off if we didn't spy on you an' report back to 'im. Normally we wouldn't believe such an unimaginable threat, even from 'im, but then, then . . ." she broke off as she became choked with tears.

"Then he punished another fairy that works fer him," finished Beloit, "and actually cut off her wings." Here he exchanged a look with his sister that nearly broke Lily's heart.

"Oh, you poor things," she said, kneeling down so she could be nearer them. "Isn't there anyone who could protect you?"

Beloit shot her a hot look. "You mean because we're so **small**??" Marzipan took his hand in her own and gave the princess a defiant look.

"Oh no, I'm sorry, I didn't mean to offend," Lily sputtered as Beloit sadly shook his head at her. "I just meant, can't his servants band together, unionize maybe, or is he cruel to all of you, hm?" she finished lamely.

"I'm afraid he is," answered Marzipan. "He's got everyone so terrified of 'im, there's really nuffing we can do. 'Cept maybe run away," she added.

"Run away. . . ." Lily echoed thoughtfully, mind racing with possible ways to protect them. "Oh!" she exclaimed after a moment. "You could stay here!"

Marzipan's blue eyebrows came together over her nose, while Beloit's earth-colored ones reached for his mossy hairline, both expressions of doubt and surprise.

"I don't see as that'll help us. He'll only get suspicious when we're missin', and he knows we've come up here –" protested Marzipan.

"Don't be ridiculous, we can be smarter than him, we'll think of something," she assured them. "In fact, we can ask the Book of Enlightenment. It will help."

Lily turned to the chair where she had laid the Book. She flipped to the Index.

"Book, can I hide these two fairies from their master?" she asked simply.

The pages turned slowly to a section called "To See or Not To See: The Art of Keeping Secrets." A single sentence glowed:

One can always hide what is not there to be seen.

"Hmm." Lily bit her full bottom lip in thought. The Book was not as clear as it usually was. She'd have to sort it out for herself.

"Well," she began slowly, ". . . this must mean that if you stay with me, you won't be around the prince for him to see. So that settles it. I'll rescue you from him."

"But m'lady," began Beloit, but stopped. His mouth hung open, and nothing came out.

"We couldn't possibly impose on yer highness," said Marzipan with a nervous chuckle.

"Of course it's not an imposition, don't be silly. I'm saving your wings."

Marzipan looked dumbly at her brother, who shrugged his shoulders up to his pointy ears.

"Now, we must find a place to hide you till the prince leaves," Lily began, pacing again.

"The prince!" exploded Beloit. "The prince is still 'ere, m'lady, askin' fer your hand. You may be able ta hide us fer now," he gestured to count himself and Marzipan, "but ya don't know as you might have ta marry him. Then we'd all end up in 'is clutches."

Lily stopped mid-pace to frown. "I hadn't thought of that," she muttered. She shook her head as if to clear it, making waves with her dark brown hair. "No, my father wouldn't pick him, if he's as awful as you say. And even if he did, he'll tell me first and I can tell him to pick someone else." She smiled faintly, with a question in her delicate eyebrows.

"Beggin' your pardon, princess," said Marzipan, "but your father din't tell you he was even *looking* fer a husband for you. You had ta find out from us."

Lily had no response to this. There *were* a lot of white horses out there in the courtyard. No one had even come to tell her about it, not even Martha.

"Then I must speak to the king. Right away." She couldn't mention the fairies of course, but perhaps she could simply say that she'd heard about this prince's cruelty from one of his servants. She was turning over various phrases and simple lies in her mind when suddenly the door swung open.

"Oh my lady!" exclaimed Martha from the doorway. "I was just coming to fetch you. There are all sorts of suitors downstairs, all for you, and they've all brought flowers –" Martha rambled breathlessly.

"Yes, I know about the suitors. Come in, shut the door. Martha, I'd like you to meet Marzipan and Beloit." She gestured to the fairies hovering waist high in the middle of the small room, with as much grand ceremony as she felt was needed at this momentous moment. Martha noticed them for the first time and gasped.

The lady took a few hesitant steps closer, staring widely. Finally she said, almost in a whisper, "I haven't seen one of you since, well, since before her highness was born. I kept a book from my childhood with drawings of fairies in it, because I wanted to remember our garden fairies after they'd gone." Her eyes turned toward Beloit. "One of 'em had hair the picture of yours."

Marzipan and Beloit looked at each other for a long moment, some unspoken comment passing between them.

"Ain't you never seen a fairy before, princess?" asked Marzipan.

"Never. My father banned them from my kingdom." Her eyes shone as she looked from one fairy to the other, as if she couldn't get enough of them.

"Hmph. Well this day suddenly got more interesting," muttered Beloit.

"These fairies are servants to one of the suitors. Come, I'll explain on the way. I must speak to my father at once." Lily took Martha's elbow to steer her out the door.

"I'm afraid that's not possible," said Martha, not budging. "I've come to take you to get dressed. You're to be presented to the gallery in an hour."

"I don't care about dressing for the gallery," said Lily impatiently. "We'll speak to the king first."

"No," Martha shook her head again. "The king is already entertaining the guests. He gave me strict instructions to see you dressed and escorted to dinner, and you can't possibly be seen by all those noble sirs until you've been properly attired and presented."

Lily's mouth hung open but nothing came out, most unbecoming of a princess. Before she could think of anything to say, any way out of it, Martha was hustling her out and down the stairs and shepherding the fairies out behind her. Lily still could think of nothing as she was led down the spiraling stairs, the Book of Enlightenment dangling from her hands.

Part Four
In which Princess Lily Goes to a Party

B y the time Princess Lily, her maid Martha, and the fairies Marzipan and Beloit reached the royal dressing chamber, Lily had regained her voice and cobbled to-gether a loose plan. She could not be seen by the noblemen without being presented, so she sent Martha to the king with the message his daughter needed to speak to him urgently before the presentation. In the meantime, Lily would dress with the help of her other twelve ladies-in-waiting (Martha was only her favorite). She insisted the fairies remain with her, so they would not fall back into the clutches of the detestable Prince Alexander of Sweethaven, or be seen accidentally by the king.

Martha returned a short while later as the ladies were putting the ninth and final layer of undergarments on Lily before her gown of caramel satin and gold chiffon.

"What did he say?" asked Lily, her voice muffled by the chemise being pulled over her head. "Is he coming to speak to me?" Her head popped out of the top of the garment and her green eyes were wide.

Martha sighed and crossed her hands in front of her, in a posture of Bad News. "I'm afraid not, your highness."

"But why not???" shrieked Lily, panic and frustration colliding in her voice.

"He's too busy with the visitors," said Martha, putting up her hands in a calming gesture. "He's been plied with drink by the men trying to impress him, and they are all doing their best to be gallant and dashing and kind, and all those sorts of things a Perfect Prince is supposed to be. His Majesty says that whatever you've got to say is less important than the matter at hand, which is to say finding you a husband. Which he is doing right now, so you will have to wait until after." Martha took a deep breath and added, "I am sorry, m'lady."

Lily stared at Martha in disbelief for a moment as one maid combed her hair, another buffed her nails, a third slipped a stocking on her left foot, and yet another powdered her face which made the look of disbelief a trifle dusty.

"Well," she said finally, "was he talking with Prince Alexander? I mean maybe we're getting upset over nothing if he's not even in Papa's inner circle."

Martha thought for a second before replying. "I really didn't catch any of their names. There were so many of them." She smiled suddenly, a brown bird ruffling her wings. "Think of it this way – you'll certainly have your pick of husbands. Many are really very handsome."

"The problem is whether I'm the one who gets to do the picking," Lily muttered. "Marzipan," she called into the antechamber where the fairies were being guarded from harm. "Marzipan, what does your master the prince look like?"

Marzipan fluttered through the doorway on her blue and white wings. "He's big, and a bit fat, and he's greazy brown curls. He's a harrible stutter, 'cept when he's angry. He generally smells of cabbage or horse manure – he's got a lot in common wiv that mount of his, let me tell ya. His eyes are very dark, almost squinky. His nose is rather dull –"

"Yes, that'll do. Thank you, Marzi," Lily interrupted, dismissing her with a brief smile. "Anyone resembling that, Martha?"

"Ooh," Martha scrunched up her freckled nose, "one or two maybe. Most of 'em are so lovely, I din't look at the fat ones." She shrugged.

"Well, I suppose if he was a favorite of Papa's you'd have noticed." She sighed and looked at herself in the mirror (not the magical one). She was radiant in the gold and caramel brown, all her color coming out in her cheeks, her eyes a shade darker than the brown of the dress. Her thirteen ladies cooed and primped and complimented her loveliness. Lily took no notice of them.

"I must look at the Book again before we go down," she

said, gathering the tome in her arms. Her question was quick and to the point: "How can I keep the king from choosing Prince Alexander to be my husband?" "Choosing a Husband, p. 93" appeared in the Index. The pages began to flutter, turning and turning deeper into the Book.

A knock on the door produced an impatient queen. "It is time, my daughter, for you to meet your suitors."

Lily held up one hand with the index finger extended to indicate her mother must wait. The pages fluttered faster. Almost there.

But the queen had had enough. "We won't be waiting for the ink to dry. Time for you to get your head out of that book, today of all days." She grabbed the Book out of Lily's hands, ignoring her protests, and set it on the table. She took Lily's hands to lead her out of the room. Before she was dragged away, Lily saw a single word float magically off the page that lay open: "*Persephone*".

The gallery was a long narrow balcony that spanned one entire wall of the Absolutely Most Grand Hall where the royal family stood to address an audience. As Lily walked with her parents up to the gallery, the minstrels stopped playing, the trumpeters sounded a fanfare, and the royal crier announced them to the awaiting court.

"King William Henry Starling the 5th, together with his queen, Elizabeth Alero Allegra, wish to present their only heir and daughter, Her Highness, the Princess Lily Rose Violet Starling, to this company here assembled. Hear ye and pay homage to their Majesty."

Lily was assailed by a wave of applause and cheers as she came to stand at the rail of the gallery. So many people filled the hall, many more than she expected. Of course there were the usual courtiers, all of whom had attendants, and the princes and dukes and earls and the one king each had an entourage of his own, but still Lily expected a few dozen suitors at best.

"Just how many are they?" she asked her mother out of the corner of her mouth as she waved to the crowd.

"Fifty-six by last count, and it's possible more have arrived in the few minutes I was gone to get you," said the queen out of the opposite corner of her own mouth. "You will certainly have your choice of husbands." She smiled at her daughter with pleasure. Lily's heart skipped a little and she felt suddenly lighter, as this echoed what Martha had said in the dressing chamber. Perhaps she would get to choose. And anyway, Prince Alexander would have some stiff competition.

She scanned the audience for the slimy fellow the fairies had described. Martha was right, many of them were quite spectacular. Some were swarthy with dark hair and beards, others tall and broad and red as Vikings ready for some happy pillaging. Blonds of all sizes dappled the hall like sunlight on the forest floor. All in all, there were a great many big shoulders, white smiles, finely-chiseled jaw lines. From where Lily stood, it looked to be a splendid party.

The first half hour of strolling the hall escorted by her father was a dizzy blur for our princess. As you may know, back in olden times, people did not really "date" much, especially not royal ladies like the Princess Lily. In some cultures they did get to meet their betrothed before marrying at least, and probably share a lunch or two, but this was all done under the scrutiny of king-dads and queen-mums who had initiated the whole mating ritual. So although our princess was already 15, she was terribly inexperienced when it came to men. Of course, she'd been told her whole life that she was beautiful, charming, incomparable, and all those other fabulous words by which you have come to know her. Just like any Jane, Jill, or Harriet, she knew what she found appealing on instinct even without experience. But imagine being swarmed by 59 (indeed the number *had* gone up since last count) 59 royal and noble men, each complimentary and well-mannered and doing everything he could to impress you in the five minutes he had before you had to move on to the next guy who would do everything *he* could to impress you. Well, I'm sure you can understand why Lily felt overwhelmed and muddled and as if she didn't know whether to laugh or run out of the room flailing her arms like a madwoman.

Now I have described most of her suitors as yummy and scrumptious, and most of them were, but the truth is the yummy scrumptious ones were not usually the most interesting. After she got over that initial breathlessness upon introduction, before the five minutes were up, the gorgeous gentleman almost always had time to say something daft about sword fighting being better than reading any day, or insult fairies, home gnomes and other little folk.

Prince Carlton of East Cloudland, for instance, was snazzily dressed and not bad looking with sharp green eyes, a quick ironic smirk, and black curls that were striking, if unfortunately puffy.

"I have been eagerly anticipating finally making your acquaintance, your Highness," he intoned, bending over her hand and batting black eyelashes before getting around to bestowing a kiss. "I am delighted to find that the richness of your beauty is equal to the richness of your kingdom."

Lily smiled as she retrieved her hand, aware of the poetic compliment but not sure if he was proper to have mentioned money so eagerly. "I'm delighted you decided it was worth coming all the way from East Cloudland. How are you finding our kingdom of Starling? Have you had any time to enjoy our countryside?"

"Not yet, but I'm certain I shall make time for it. Yours is a lush landscape of rich hunting ground, and I have been wanting to visit it for just that purpose for some time. I love nothing more than to hunt boar, and hunt deer, and hunt pheasant, and small game, large game, really anything in between, too, for that matter!" His lips curled up charmingly on one side in amusement at his own wit. Even as she admired his smile, Lily was not sure whether he was truly happy to meet her or simply wanted to swing by Castle Starling on his way through the neighborhood. "In fact," Prince Carlton continued, "the gift I brought you is a perfect example of how important hunting is to me, and how important I find it is to dress perfectly for all my hunting trips."

He seemed so eager to tell her about himself, she could hardly help but ask: "What is it that you've brought me?"

"A truffle pig! Have you ever seen them in action? No? Oh, they are excellent hunters, and this one is my favorite from my brood at home. Absolutely brilliant at finding truffles, which are the most expensive delicacy imaginable. It's all part of the gift. Maximillian would be so pleased with the way he's being presented."

"Maximillian?"

"The pig. Name's Maximillian. That's how grand I thought of him, with his one-in-a-million nose for truffles."

"Well," said the princess, slightly bewildered at the strangeness of the gift of a pig, but intrigued and flattered nonetheless, "I look forward to taking Maximillian truffle hunting. Tell me, why does this unusual gift show how you like hunting dress, though?"

"Because of how the pig is dressed!" His ironic smirk made another appearance and he winked one green eye at her. "That's Maximillian over there!"

He pointed one long silk-clad arm across the room, where a large pig was hanging on a spit through its body and out its mouth, dainty cloven toes dangling. Its eyes had been replaced with roasted cherries, and a garland of spices and garlic festooned its neck. The hide was glistening with juices, having been perfectly roasted, and the crowning achievement of the dressing, Prince Carlton explained, was that it was stuffed with the last marvelous haul of truffles the great hunter had ever found.

The selfish, arrogant Carlton with his selfish, horrifying gift was the worst of the good-looking but not good guys in the Starling court. There were a few gorgeous guys who managed not to say anything idiotic, and there were a few brilliant personalities who came in an older, or squintier, or jowl-heavier package.

Of course you only want to hear about Prince Alexander. Sorry to keep you waiting. Just wanted a little backdrop for his entrance, as Lily had, because he was the very last person she met that night.

The presentation and the strolling introductions and the feast and then the ball were all a bit too much for the princess and she slipped out into the corridor for a few moments of peace and quiet. She leaned against a wall wondering at all the events of the night, all the people she had met, and all the new feelings and ideas she now had about how one went about choosing a husband. After a very short while pondering, she sank under the ponderous weight of it onto a small cushioned bench, near one of the end tables which held a bouquet of lilies, roses, and violets.

"Are you feeling faint, my lady? You don't seem quite well." A dark-haired male courtier appeared at her elbow, soft thick eyebrows raised in concern. Her glazed vision passed over him, and managed to fix on his dark deep-set eyes for a moment. Lily had nothing to say after so many hours of smiling and laughing and being charming right back at these noblemen. She simply looked this man in the eye for a minute and then dumbly shook her head.

He smiled at her and brought her a glass of water, along with a handkerchief he produced from his sleeve.

Lily accepted both politely but quietly. He remained standing next to her but didn't talk.

After a few minutes and the last swallow of water, Lily felt glad for his kindness. "Thank you very much. So much more refreshing than the wine. I needed that." She smiled faintly up at him.

One corner of his mouth quirked up pleasantly. "Yes, that Quattro Centro stuff they're serving tonight can feel very heavy after the third glass."

"Certainly can," replied Lily, looking back down into her empty glass. Apparently this servant drank the same wine as his master. "I know I'm the reason for all this, but I suddenly feel as if I weren't Princess Lily at all, that this is all about someone else. I imagine they won't even miss me for a while. They've all moved on to their fourth and fifth glasses of Quattro Centro and reverted to bragging to my father."

The young man held a hand up to Lily for a second and discreetly peeked around the corner into the Absolutely Most Grand Hall. "I think you're safe," he said coming back to her. "They're all in their cups, as you said. Looks like your father is too, though. I saw a whole gang of them around him when we arrived, all wanting to show off for him. Trying to impress the wrong end of the royal family, if you ask me."

Lily tilted her head to one side curiously. "What do you mean by that? You think the queen will get a bigger vote?"

The young man tilted his head in return, and sank down onto the bench beside her. "I mean you, my lady."

Lily's smile was genuine this time. Blushing, she turned away from him to fidget with the gold cording on her dress. "I only hope to have veto power, even if they do choose for me. There are some terrible men in this lot."

"Well, I know some of them are twits. So many seem to think they were clever to bring flowers in your name. At least we were able to employ a scribe for the gift we brought. And I'll grant you, some that aren't daft do have unpleasant personal habits," he made an exaggerated grimace here that made Lily laugh, "but most of them are decent enough."

"Oh no, I don't just mean the neck hair on Sir Dahlinghurst or Prince Carlton's hunting obsession. There's at least one man here who is truly evil. I have it on good word that he is downright abusive to his servants. I can only imagine what he'd do to a wife," Lily said gravely.

"Really? I don't think any of the chaps I know are like that." Lily marveled at how casually this servant talked of his superiors. "Besides, you don't know what the servants are like. Some of them do tend to make things sound worse than reality, so their masters take it easy on them. It is *possible* that you aren't hearing the whole truth," he added gently when he saw the stern look on her face.

"Truly, I have heard rightly. These are loyal servants of a prince who makes them perform devious and dishonorable tasks, all the while holding threat of bodily harm over them. They've even seen a fellow servant maimed by the prince himself," Lily's voice rose in horror, her eyes getting darker by the second.

"Maimed??" he asked in some alarm. "What sort of punishment was afflicted on them? And who is this prince?"

"He had a fairy's wings cut off, and threatened to do the same to my friends. His name is –"

"Wait," he interrupted, laying his hand on Lily's forearm. "You're talking about fairy servants? Princess, you have been terribly misguided. You can't possibly believe whatever rubbish they're telling you. Certain little folk are not the least trustworthy. You may be able to call on them for certain things, but telling the truth is **not** one of them."

Lily spoke through her teeth now. "I caught them in my reading room where they were sent by their master to spy on me. And I saw the tears in Marzipan's eyes when she told me about his punishments." She wrenched her arm violently from his grip.

But the man had let go as if her arm was on fire, his eyes going wide in shock. "Marzipan? Did you say the fairy's name was Marzipan? Why on earth would she say such things about her prince?" This last question was as if to himself.

"You know her. You must work for Prince Alexander, too. Surely you've witnessed some of his cruelty, even if he's not as bad to other humans." Now it was Lily's turn to approach him, anger melting into sympathy.

But the man's face just seemed unable to let go of its shocked look. He stared at Lily as if she had grown another head and didn't say anything comforting.

"What a stupid girl...." he muttered as he ran his hands through his dark curls.

"Ah, there you are, Lily," came the voice of the king from the entrance to the hall. "We've been looking for you to complete the introductions." He walked toward the couple. When he was a few feet away, he said, "But I can see you've already met your final suitor, Prince Alexander of Sweethaven."

Lily stared at her father, who was smiling brightly, and

turned with deliberate slowness to the man sitting next to her. The prince still ruffled his dark curls, so that when he looked up at her, they were sticking up.

It was finally he who broke the silence. "Honestly, your highness, you've got it all wrong. Those fairies are lying to you completely. If you knew them –"

"I do know them!" replied Lily hotly, springing to her feet. "And I know you for what you are, you lying skull. Here you were pretending to be a servant all this while!"

"I never said I was a servant!" exploded the prince. "You made your own assumptions about me. And as for the fairies, if you had even read about them, you'd know that Marzipan and Beloit's tribe are notorious mischief-makers akin to brownies."

"I am very well read!" shouted the princess. "And I don't ever plan to be locked in a tower or thrown in an oubliette for reading!" Lily spun on her heel, facing the king again, and began stomping past him down the hallway.

"Oh, you must be joking!" shouted the prince.

"Now really, sweet pea, calm down," chimed in the king, spinning around to follow her.

At the entrance to the hall, Lily was stopped short by a near collision with the queen, coming out to continue the search for the AWOL princess. Before she knew it, she was caught in a triangle between her parents and her would-be husband.

"What's going on?" asked the queen. After several minutes of shouting and interrupting and no-no-noing, the queen gathered the gist of the fray. Quieting everyone with her calm but insistent demeanor, the queen said it was quite clear they'd gotten off on the wrong foot and suggested they return to the hall to start over with a nice glass of wine.

Lily protested at the top of her lungs again, saying they should throw Prince Alexander out on his ear. At this, the king spoke up.

"I know you've got a bad idea about this man, but I'm certainly not going to throw him out on the word of some **fairies**. I don't care how excited you are to finally meet some, but you've taken it to an extreme to believe such a tale. Besides, there's more at stake here than you, my dear sweet pea. Sweethaven has huge tracts of land and I have the future of our kingdom to think about."

All three people looked at Princess Lily. The prince had said nothing through her latest rant and now looked at her with a mixture of annoyance and something else – disappointment? regret? Whatever it was, it wasn't shame. The king and queen wore duplicate parental looks that said 'dare and contradict us,' which after such a long night was hard for Lily to imagine doing.

She deeply regretted letting her father know about the fairies, but her plans for deception had been overthrown by her passion in the argument with Prince Alexander. She came to a decision. "Of course you're right, your Majesty. I am sorry. We can sit down together. But first," she looked up pleadingly to her mother and father in turn, "could I have Martha take me to freshen up a little? It has been a long night and looks to go on even longer, and I would like to make the best *second* impression on Prince Alexander that I can."

The king and queen looked delighted at this change in their daughter's attitude, though the prince looked surprised. If they had paused to look closer, they would have seen her eyes remained molasses brown.

"Pour the wine without me. I will join you shortly," she said, taking her leave with a small bow.

Martha met her on the stairway. "The queen says you are recovering from a headache, m'lady. Shall I bring you a tonic while you freshen up?"

"That won't be necessary, Martha. I've left the headache behind." A queer smile came over her, and when she gave Martha a sidelong glance, the brown eyes did not escape the handmaiden's notice.

"Oh dear," muttered Martha.

"Would you go up to my chamber ahead of me and see that the other ladies are all away? I want only you and the fairies when I come up so that I may have a few moments of peace."

"Yes, m'lady," said Martha with a sigh, hiking her skirts and sprinting up the stairs.

When Lily got there, she went straight to her wardrobe and began throwing things out into the room in a hurry. She moved on to the shelves when she seemed satisfied with the pile of clothing. She picked up the magic mirror, the ever-dancing shoes, and the magic firebrands. The fairies and handmaiden looked on, and finally Marzipan spoke.

"What are you planning to do, princess?"

Lily smiled as she pulled her hair out of its ribbons and braided it tightly in a single club. "I'm taking the advice I gave you, Marzipan. I'm running away, and you're coming with me. That way, we won't be here to be seen by Prince Alexander," she spoke a little breathlessly with excitement, "will we?"

Part Five
In which Begins a Journey to a Distant Land

"**I**t's the only thing that makes sense," said Princess Lily to her servant Martha and the fairies Marzipan and Beloit as she packed clothes into a canvas bag. "I can't possibly stay here when there's a chance my parents will make me marry that awful prince. It's clear they don't care what I think. Besides, I've sworn to protect the fairies, and now that he knows they're with me, he's bound to try to reclaim them. I know you don't want to think about what he would do to you," she said to Marzipan and Beloit.

They looked at her and then at each other for a moment. "She's right," said Beloit quietly. "You know we can't go back, Marzi. Our best chance is wiv her."

Marzipan put her hands on the hips of her overalls, and flew to eye level in front of the princess. "You met the prince? Our Prince Alexander?"

"Yes," said Lily, "outside the Hall when I was taking a breather. I thought he was a servant at first. It seemed like he was being rather kind to me, talking to me like a person rather than a ... a flatterer or a braggart or a farmer at a market." She looked away from Marzipan, fiddled with the things she was packing.

Martha chuckled a little at this. When Lily shot her a look, she shrugged. "He sounds better than a lot of them. Maybe he's not that bad after all."

Marzipan flew into Lily's field of vision again. "What made you change your mind about him?"

Lily paused a moment before answering, anger flaring back anew. "He said horrible things about servants. Fairies in particular." She looked from Marzipan to Beloit. "He called me stupid for listening to you. He insulted your tribe, and said you were lying to me."

Beloit flew over to join his sister. Marzipan seemed to understand then, and she nodded to him. "Then you saw for yourself how awful he is," he said. "Just b'cause a fellow's charmin' at first, doesn't mean he's not a pig. We'll go wiv you, princess." Beloit flew over and kissed her left cheek.

"Yeah, we'll come wiv you," said Marzipan, who kissed her other cheek. Lily sighed with excitement.

Martha stood up suddenly. "Are you sure you want to take such rash action, princess?"

Lily stopped packing, holding a bundle of clothes in her hand and looking sharply at Martha. She was not accustomed to her favorite maid second-guessing her.

"You'd be giving up your entire life here, leaving your family and friends, the only home you've ever known. All your lovely clothes and your magical collection. Possibly your crown. All because of a story told you by some fairies you've known less than a day."

Lily shook her head and huffed, turning away to stuff the clothes into her pack. "You sound like my father."

"Well ... maybe your father has a point!" Martha, most of the time so pleasant, agreeable and placid, spoke to her mistress harshly for the first time either of them could remember. "I'm not saying the fairies aren't telling the truth. I don't rightly know. I do know you're more likely to believe them over the prince, or the king, or even me, because you've always harbored such affection for fairies. Even say their story is true. You don't know for sure that your parents will pick their prince. Sounds to me like you've mortally offended him anyway. Perhaps he's decided not court you after that. There are 56 men down at court –"

"Fifty-nine," corrected Lily petulantly, sitting on the edge of her bed.

"Great, then, 59 suitors all together. Don't any of the rest of them deserve a chance? Why throw away everything because of the one stinker out of 59?" When the princess did not reply, she sat down on the bed next to her. "Wait till tomorrow and see how it lies. Don't go back to the party tonight when you're so upset. Sleep on it. In the morning, things may seem different, or the king may have more to say, to put your mind at ease."

The princess took a moment to compare her excitement over the journey with everything she was leaving behind, and search her feelings over her situation. "It's so scary, Martha. So frightening to think about what that man could do to Marzipan and Beloit. And what he could do to me if he were my husband. I can't stop imagining it!"

"Scarier than being out on your own in a strange world? Scarier than ruffians and highwaymen and wolves in the woods?"

After a long moment, Lily nodded. Martha squeezed her with one arm, acquiescing.

"I'll find a place to be safe, Martha. Once I see the fairies have escaped him for good, I'll send word back to you, and see if I can come home. I just know that my father and mother will take my objection seriously then. Until I'm gone, I'll be afraid every moment."

Martha nodded. "What can I do to help, my lady?"

The princess gathered the last of her things into the pack, stuffing the Book of Enlightenment in last. "I want you to go to the kitchen and get as much food as you can sneak away, enough to fill a saddlebag. Make sure no one sees you. Meet us in the stables at the south end of the Rose Vine Courtyard. We're going to find us a horse."

Princess Lily chose a route down from her bedroom to the stables where she was least likely to be seen. The back staircase was the one the servants used when hauling linens and things up to the beds, baths, and beyond, and empty dishes down to the kitchen. These were chores for midday when beds were empty and the royal residents and guests were about their business, but there was far too much other work to be done during a feast. Lily had no trouble sneaking down to the courtyard, though she did it with much tip-toeing and slow peeking around every corner.

Lily was not surprised (and neither will you be, if you recall what the Book of Enlightenment predicted) to see the courtyard was filled with fog, so dense she could barely see five feet in front of her. It was as thick as cream of tomato soup (which is a few gradients thinner than the more famous pea soup fog, but slightly thicker than minestrone fog). Nonetheless, to be safe, the fairies went through the courtyard as scouts, small enough to escape notice, and whistled to Lily when the coast was clear. Lily wore her archery dress which was a light wool in dark green, the better for hunting with and sneaking in the dark. Her bow was strapped to her back with its quiver and her full pack.

Lily felt a bit dazzled when she entered the stable and walked down its clean-swept aisles past white horse after white horse. "They all look alike," she said. "How will we pick a good one? A nice, fast, quiet horse who won't cause us trouble getting away?"

Marzipan and Beloit floated past the stalls with indifference, but then Lily noticed they had stopped in front of one stall and were talking excitedly together. "What is it? Have you found a good one?"

"Yes, princess," said Beloit as she neared the stall, a great grin on his teeny face. "He looks like a dandy. Sturdy and quiet, and he sure stands out from the rest."

Lily leaned over the door of the stall Beloit pointed out, and saw a chestnut gelding, which is another way of saying a male horse dark brown in color who can't get a girlfriend, his shiny black eyes calmly staring back at Lily. When the horse saw her looking at him, he softly ambled toward her across the short distance from the other side of the stall. He rubbed his velvety nose gently on Lily's outstretched hand. Not knowing much about horses, Lily took this as a friendly gesture rather than the request for an apple the horse had meant to convey.

"Ooh, he's lovely!" she said. "He's perfect for running away on. Er, riding away, aren't you?" She continued to rub his nose and tilted her head as she asked this silly question. The horse snorted and bobbed his head up and down, in what looked like agreement, but was really a question about ripe, round, red fruit. "We should have just enough time to saddle him before

Martha returns with our supplies."

Indeed, Lily was tugging on the last cinch, with lots of instruction from Marzipan who *had* spent time around horses, just as Martha sneaked into the stable with the food. She just made it to the stall before dropping any of her linen-wrapped packages.

"Splendid job, Martha. We'll be set for at least a week." Lily picked up the apple that had tumbled out of Martha's arms, and fed it to her steed.

"Oh, there's plenty here to feed one human and two fairies, my lady," replied Martha. "You shouldn't need to buy any food for almost a fortnight."

"Buying food!" Lily smacked herself in the forehead. "Oh, Martha, I didn't even think about money! I packed some magical artifacts and a few of my necklaces I didn't want to leave behind...." Lily gazed with worry at the full saddlebags. "I suppose I could sell them in a town when it comes to it...."

"Don't even think of it, my lady." Martha was already untying a purse from her waistband. "For one thing, you're sure to be recognized if you try to sell them. Besides, I'd hate to see you give up your beautiful things, if they're to be your only comfort away from home." She took Lily's hand and put the bag into it, curling Lily's fingers around it.

"No, Martha, I couldn't possibly take this, this is your money," protested Lily. Martha just shook her head, and took her hands away, hearing none of it.

"You need it now more than I do. You'll be alone out there, save for your new friends, and have to keep you fed and warm. I'm fed and warm every day here, and I don't need any more trinkets."

Suddenly Lily realized what Martha was saying. "Alone? You mean you're not coming with me?"

Martha tilted her pretty brown head judiciously to one side. "Ah. No, my lady. I'm afraid runnin' away is not in my nature. All my life has been spent in this county, within sight of this castle, if not almost every day inside it. I can't imagine being away from it, without good reason," she added, "as you have."

Lily paused, thinking that everything Martha said also applied to her. She nearly gave up and went back inside then, so frightening was the idea of leaving without her companion that she hadn't even considered it. But no, she had to go. Lives were at stake. Including her own.

"Of course, you must decide for yourself. Once I leave this castle I'm no longer a princess, and you're no longer my servant."

Martha smiled. "P'raps you'd better think about disguising yourself, once you're around people. Use those clothes you packed and your wits to make yourself less . . . remarkable." She plucked a strand of Lily's dark brown hair and smiled, more sadly this time.

At the far end of the stable they could suddenly hear someone singing. A dark shadow fell on the hay-strewn floor as the voice got louder. The warbling was happy, louder than it should have been at that time of night, and not without its pleasant qualities. The singer lifted a lantern and sang a bright hello to the horse in the stall nearest the door.

Martha and Lily could clearly see his face as the lantern pushed the darkness aside: Gerald, the head groom. He turned toward them, noticing them for the first time, and just in time Lily pulled up her hood and turned her head aside as Martha turned to face him square on.

"Martha?" asked Gerald with mild surprise. "What you doing out here in the middle of the party?"

Without missing a beat, Martha said, "Running silly errands for one of the royals, what else?" She sounded so bored and ordinary that Lily momentarily wondered if she often felt annoyed by the tasks she gave her. "One of the princes insisted his horse needs a walk before midnight. He says it keeps the animal limber and he wants to make sure he can show his riding skills off to Starlings in the morn."

Gerald's plain, sun-tanned face screwed up. "Horses should be sleeping right now, not being ridden."

"I told him that, but d'you think they listen to me? It was

easier just to get it done and over with than to argue with him."

He shrugged at this. "Still, you came out here. Maybe you could tell him you gave the horse a witching-hour walk, but actually give the poor beast the night off, eh?" Gerald worked with horses every day and generally had more affection for them than for people.

Lily gripped the reins of the brown horse tightly. She couldn't turn and order him away as she normally would have done as a princess. She was terrified of being recognized. If he knew she was out here, surely he would tell in the morning after they knew she was gone, putting the king and evil prince on her heels before she got very far. For that matter, if she was caught now, she might never get to leave in the first place. This might be the shortest escape in history.

Martha stepped closer to Gerald and whispered, loud enough for Lily to still hear, "I get ya, man, I do, but this here is the prince's niece. He sent her to do the walking herself. I'm only here to see her to the stables, foreign castle and all. Can't very well pretend in front of her."

Gerald looked at Lily's back and grunted. He didn't like so many strangers milling about in the stables, his little kingdom. "Alright. You sure you don't need any help getting it saddled and all, miss?"

Lily patted the horse's withers and shook her cloaked head emphatically.

"Doesn't talk much, does she?"

"No," said Martha, "thankfully. Say, have you gotten to try that Quattro Centro wine yet? It's really good stuff, better than what we usually get." She casually stepped out of the stable door, making Gerald back up a few steps and then walk beside her so he wouldn't be rude. Lily heard their voices recede into the courtyard. She saw the fairies safely into a warm compartment in the saddlebags, opened the stall and led the horse out by the reins through the near door.

She kept her head down as she walked, neither fast nor slow, toward the castle gates. She was just wondering if she had seen her friend and closest ally for the last time when Martha appeared again.

"I've got him set up with some of the strongest wine inside. Here's hoping he won't remember even going out to the stables by the morning." They embraced and said their I-shall-miss-yous. Lily mounted the horse.

"Where will you go?" asked Martha, looking up at her.

Lily took a deep breath before answering. "All I can think is to look for a lady called Persephone. That's the name that the Book said. I haven't time to consult it now. I will as soon as we're well away from the castle. For now I head south, and hope I find this wisewoman."

Through the mist they could just see that the gate in the castle wall was open, due to all the guests, so Lily pulled the hood of her cloak closer around her face again, kicked the horse once, and bolted through the gate and onto the road.

South down the road away from the castle, galloping through the village, darkness touching her face, the wind reaching cold fingers inside her cloak, fog closing around her like a garment that is too tight, Lily rode the horse hard through the first night. Sometime several hours later, it began to rain, washing the mist down into the earth. Twas always a blessing to have rain only at night before, but it made this night seem bleaker to our princess. Her cloak kept her dry, as it was made of fine stuff, but the wind would not leave off poking her.

As the sun rose, Lily began to look for a place to rest. The country was wooded with low rolling hills, just like Lily's home. In fact, they hadn't even left the kingdom of Starling yet. Lily pressed the horse up a rise to the west of the road, and tried not to think on it.

A rocky outcropping in the woods on the hill provided some cover, so Lily dismounted and woke the fairies before unsaddling the horse. Over a breakfast of fruit and bread, the fairies proposed all sorts of adventures.

"Have you e'rer seen the singin' trees in the forest of Gesundheit?" mumbled Beloit around a mouthful of apple.

"Heard 'em, I mean. They're most amazing when you put your ear t' their trunks and hum a tune. They always know the words."

"That's right!" joined in Marzipan. "R'member the time we got a whole grove o' them singin' 'One million goblets of ale on the wall'? It went on for *days*!"

"Weeks!" shouted Beloit.

Lily shook with laughter, nearly dropping her bread in the dirt.

"That's the problem wiv singin' trees," said Marzipan when she'd regained her breath. "They have ta finish a song once they start it. Can't be distracted."

"Very obsessive, singing trees," agreed Beloit, nodding his head meditatively.

"But where is this Gesundheit kingdom? You've both been there?" Lily asked. As the sun was finally up, she pulled the Book out of her pack so she could look at a map.

"Oh yeh, me and sis've been all over the place."

Lily lay on her belly and flipped through the Book. "So you haven't always been servants? How long have you been in Prince Alexander's employ?"

After a long pause, Beloit said, "About five years. We worked fer 'is family before him."

"Well, you two must be old enough to remember your home –"

"Only about a 'undred years old," muttered Marzipan.

"Oh," said Lily, "of course, fairies live a long time. I knew I'd read that. So what was life like before you went to Sweethaven?"

"Our tribe is from the southern borders of Sweethaven. We're Soula-Mays," said Beloit. "Our grand and noble people are best known fer their feasts and balls. Every Beltane, Lunasadh, Samhain, Imbolc, Hogmany, and Kasimir Polaski Day, we have feasts that last a week, startin' and endin' wiv a grand ball. Pretty much t' rest of the year is put into plannin' the parties."

"My favorite part is the fashion," said Marzipan. "Seein' the new styles for the year in every possible natural material, feathers and leaves and flower buds and acorn caps, seeds and sprouts, sometimes birch bark. And everyone looks so lovely as they dance, and tell stories, and promenade, and sing."

"And light the fires," put in Beloit.

"Yes, the fires. Fairy fires, you'd call them, but they're just plain ol' feast fires t' us. It's the gettin' dressed up and performin' I like best," she said, smiling in memory.

"Why, I never would have guessed you were so fashion-conscious, Marzi," replied Lily, looking at the girl's worn-out overalls, lavender t-shirt, and wildly uncombed, bright blue hair. "The parties sound lovely."

"My favorite part is the food," said her brother. "Daffodil cream puffs and jonquil jelly, amber beer, jasmine petit fours, and silver-grape wine. The best fried cricket and sautéed chickadee you'd ever taste was at festival time." Beloit ripped a chunk of bread with his teeth and waved the rest of it about. "Someday we'll have chickadees sautéed in butter again, Marzi."

Lily sat up and said, "You can go back now, if you like. I mean since you're no longer under the rule of that wicked prince. Once we're safely away from my kingdom, couldn't you go home?" She looked from Marzipan to Beloit and back again.

Beloit's earthy eyebrows shot up at this new idea. "Now there's an idea," he said. "I haven't thought of going home in at least a decade. What ter ya say, Marz?"

Marzipan frowned at him a moment, then she flew up to the horse's head, coming to rest in the thick dark mane. "I guess I just can't believe yet that we've really gotten away from Prince Alexander," she said, patting the chestnut horse and looking back at her brother.

"Oh yeah, right," he said flatly.

"Now don't let's get down on ourselves. So far we've gotten away clean. There's every reason to hope we'll succeed. I won't let the prince take you," said Lily fiercely.

"Hadn't we better figure out where we're off to then, m'lady?" asked Marzipan from her hairy perch.

Lily looked down into her lap, suddenly remembering the

Book. "Yes, of course," she muttered, turning from the map to the index.

"Who is Persephone?" she asked the Book.

When the pages rested, the index entries under the letter "P" glowed and hovered off the page.

> *Persephone dragon*
> *Persephone fish*
> *Persephone, janitoress of Merlin's Boot Closet*
> *Persephone, Queen of Hadesborough*
> *Persephone, underduchess of East Cloudland*
> *Persephonemesometime flower*
> *Persephotoshoppe*

"Show me, 'Persephone, Queen of Hadesborough,'" said Lily.

Pages fluttered.

> *Persephone Josephine Phoebe Phyllis the Fifth became queen of Hadesborough in the year of the Falcon upon her marriage to King Hal. Being just south of Sweethaven, Persephone's childhood home, her union with Hadesborough has caused much trouble in the region, as worries over annexation and potential damage to the pomegranate market, where both countries get a large portion of their income, seem to rise every autumn and spring.*

"Oh, there's a Persephone who came from Sweethaven," Lily said over her shoulder to the fairies. Of course she couldn't see the worried looks on their faces as she buried her dull nose in the Book.

> *Queen Persephone has been called "the greatest ruler of our time" by the editors of the Knightly Times, as they run frequent coverage of her smashing outfits worn at her Dragon Outreach Summit and her Troll Rehabilitation Benefit Feast, both of which she coordinates and hosts. "Queen P is saving the Enlightened Kingdoms from ruin and looking swell doing it," popularly quoted Sir Scandalot once said of her.*

"She sounds very diplomatic," said Lily, to the fairies who were now whizzing back and forth over the poor horse's head.

> Her diplomacy has led to her unofficial home for wayward girls in the Castle Hadesburg, where young ladies who have no home or have otherwise lost their way can stay until suitable homes or adoptive families can be found for them. This off-the-books charity is barely tolerated by King Hal, but so far the queen's goodwill has allowed her to keep the halfway castle going.

"This is perfect!" exclaimed Lily, sitting up suddenly and making her dark braid swing. "Not only will she know about Sweethaven – maybe she'll help us think up some way we can stop the torture of fairies going on there – but she's got a halfway castle for lost girls. That's me!" She tapped her chest for emphasis.

Beloit paused in his mad fluttering and hovered a moment. "You're lost?"

"Ahhp," Lily stuttered. Starting again, she said, "Well, no, I'm not lost, but I am away from home and unable to return. She sounds like rather a wise lady, and the Book says she has helped many girls."

"Tch," muttered Marzipan. "Persephone." Nobody heard her over the wild flap of her wings.

"Map, from the kingdom of Starling to Hadesborough," Lily commanded the Book. After a minute of study, she said, "It's south and east of here. Looks like we could get to the border at its western edge, close to Sweethaven. Isn't that where you said your tribe was from?"

"That's right," said Beloit without passion, "it is." He had stopped flying around and hovered near the horse's shoulder, and looked at his sister as he said this.

Marzipan was still flying in circles, now clutching her blue head. "Oh, lord, not *that* Persephone," she muttered, audibly this time. After some moments of silence, she looked up and saw

Beloit and Lily staring at her. "Look it, I've 'eard of this Persephone, an' I'm jus' not sure she's the right one. I mean," here she took a much-needed deep breath, "maybe there's other ones we should try first. Didn't yer book have some other Persephones? A janitoress?"

"Well, yes, but Queen Persephone's description sounds a lot more promising than any janitoress. Both Sweethaven and charity to lone females are mentioned," Lily pointed out.

"Oh," replied Marzipan. "It does. They are." Still whizzing in circles, though slower ones now.

"C'mon, Marzi," said Beloit, gently persuasive. "It'd be easy for us to go home, 'tis practically on the way."

The circles closed, getting smaller, slower, spiraling downward, till she finally dropped the few inches back onto the horse's mane. She lay her head down on the course brown hair for a minute. "Home. I never dreamed of going home."

"I know." Beloit came to float near her, stroking her uncontrollable hair. "But we can think about it now."

Lily, of course, had no idea why Marzipan should be so against going to Queen Persephone, and neither do you, but both she and you will just have to wait until later. She was beginning to get used to fairies reacting to things in ways she couldn't predict, so she didn't even try to understand.

Besides, it was so late it was early. She had been up since the previous morning, reading and dressing and then feasting and then drinking and then dancing and then drinking and then sitting for a moment in the hallway talking to the prince and then running and hiding and riding through the gates and riding through the night. The fairies had at least rested on the ride, but Lily was feeling even dizzier than she had coming out of the ballroom when she met our unfortunate prince.

"Anyway," she said, snapping her drooping head up, "we should get some sleep. Looks like we'll have quite a journey ahead of us, and I'm beat." Holding a fist to her yawning mouth, she dragged a bedroll and blanket off the horse's pack and fell into her makeshift bed as soon as she could, falling to sleep as soon as her head hit the saddlebag that was her pillow.

Part Six
In which the Book of Enlightenment Speaks

O ver the next few days, Lily, Marzipan, Beloit, and Milwaukee (as they had taken to calling the horse, per Beloit's idea) made their way across the countryside from twilight until the sun came up, resting when it did so. It took them three days to get out of Lily's kingdom, and until then they were very sneaky in their movements, even going so far as to hide when they heard a rider approach on the road. The fairies were a great help in this, because they would take turns flying around the next bend or up above the trees to see farther ahead on the road. Lily also remembered to keep the Book of Enlightenment out of her pack as she rode, loosely tied with a cloth in her lap, so that its Emergency Alert System would not be wasted in the saddlebag should it go off.

They began to head south towards Hades-borough and dared to spend a single night in a roadside public house. As Martha had suggested, Lily disguised herself first: she pulled her hair into a loose braid, and patted it down with reddish dust to change the color. Using her magic hairbrushes, she teased the hair out and made several small braids out of it. She found a nice patch of clay soil and wetted it with water from her flask, making a paste. With this she made a ridge that ran from one cheekbone down the side of her neck, to look like a scar. The final touch was pulling her blanket from her bedroll around her shoulders like a peasant. The magic mirror confirmed the effectiveness of the disguise, both the wishful thinking side and the inner demon side showing a girl who looked nothing like Princess Lily. They decided not to inform the innkeepers of the fairies' presence, "Just in case they're prejudiced," according to Marzipan, and because they wanted to conserve their gold.

You might think that people running for their lives ought

to have kept on sleeping in woods and under rocky outcroppings, not to even mention the cost in gold, if they wanted to continue their escape without notice. You'd probably be right, and I suggest if you are ever in a situation where you are running from an evil prince who wants to cut your wings off that you follow that instinct. But you must remember that Lily was a princess, royally born and bred, and while she had been fiercely independent most of her life, three days eating only cold food and sleeping in a bed made from a thin wool mat over grass was a real hardship for Lily. It's not that she missed being waited on hand and foot (so long as she never thought about it) or that she wanted gourmet cooking like she was used to getting at the castle, but the personal hygiene involved in roughing it was really stressing her out. *One night,* she told herself, *just to get cleaned up and well-rested and then we'll go back to hiding in the woods.* So don't be too hard on our dear princess, who was after all doing her best.

When Lily reached into the pouch of gold coins to pay the innkeeper after arranging for a room, dinner, and hot water for bathing, she was startled to feel something in the pouch that was distinctly un-coin-like. The innkeeper, an older man with a peg leg and a warm smile, didn't notice her fidgeting. When he turned to bite the coins she'd handed him and stow them in a pouch of his own, she peeked into her hand, confirming her suspicion of the not-a-coin's identity. It was a small gold ring, with a wavy green line tracing the outside. Since the coin pouch had come from Martha, it could only be the Ring of Green Dragon's Dreams. Lily stowed the ring in the purse again and tied it to her waistband.

The innkeeper brought Lily a steaming bowl of pot roast with stewed onions and potatoes, and a large mug of freshly-brewed ale. Lily savored each bite of the warm and hearty meal, never having rushed a meal in her royal life, but it was all she could do to save the last few bites for the fairies, to be given to them later in her room. As she drank her second mug of ale, the innkeeper asked of her travel plans.

"I saw you was coming fra the nort," he said. "Will you ha' been coming fra King William's kingdom, then?"

After a gulp, Lily replied, "Yes, I was wintering with my aunt in Starling, but now I go back to my father's farm for the planting," reciting the speech she'd planned as she donned her muddy disguise.

"Really?" he asked curiously. "And what sor' a crop will your father be plantin', then?"

"Pomegranates" was her quick reply, having taken a page from Persephone's book, so to speak.

"I sees. Tis it Sweethaven or Hadesborough you'll be heading home to, then?"

"It's Hadesborough, just on the western border." She couldn't stomach the idea of saying she was going to live in Sweethaven, even though it was slightly closer and thus more believable.

"Huh." The man tapped his pipe on the arm of his wooden chair, loosing charred leaves onto the stone floor with a clack-clack. "Starling to Hadesborough, now that's quite a trek. 'Specially for a woman, alone on the road." He waved his now-empty pipe at her nonspecifically. His wife appeared through a doorway behind him and swept the leaves he'd dumped into the hearth. "Doesn't 'at seem like a long way fer a young woman, Deirdre? Starling to Hadesborough? To sow pomegranates?"

"Oh, now, Alistair, leave the poor dearie alone. Tis none of our business where our guests are going," Deirdre said pleasantly, not looking up from her sweeping.

Grateful for the woman's presence that gave her time to think something up, Lily said, "Actually, I'm meeting my father on the way. Should only be another day's ride on this road and I won't be alone any longer." *That sounded pretty good, didn't it?*

"You're sure 'twouldn't be safer to stay here, then, if he's coming on this road? You could wait fer him," put in Deirdre, standing her broom against the wall and wiping her hands together.

When Lily stared at her silently working her jaw for a few

moments, the woman answered herself. "A'course, here I go, bein' nosy when I just got done telling Alistair ta leave ya alone." She waved her hand down, dismissing it. "He's only askin' where you've come from and where you're off to cuz he wants more news of Princess Lily of Starling and her flight."

Having been trained in courtly manners, and having much recent practice at smiling and acting normal no matter what sort of thing a person said to her, Lily felt sure she fooled the innkeeper and his wife with the look on her face that this just barely registered as interesting gossip. Her eyes lost a little of their green luster, however, and she felt a very hot, bubbly rock rolling around in her stomach, bumping into the pot roast.

"Well," she said slowly, picking up her mug again, "why don't you tell me what news you've got and I'll see if I know anything you haven't heard."

Alistair grinned widely as he leaned forward in his chair and packed his pipe. "We know she's run off, a'course, but nobody we've met seems ta know why, precisely. Word had gone up and down these hills and oh all over the place about the lovely princess and how rich the kingdom was getting –"

"With no little help from you, my dear husband," put in Deirdre.

Alistair ignored her and went on. "So before the king even had time to send his own word out, there was people coming from all over to meet her."

"To marry her, you mean," said Deirdre.

"So they have their big to-do, and a fuss is made, and they all get soused," – he means drunk, by the way – "everything's going along jolly good, and when the smoke clears next morning, the princess is nowhere to be found. Poof," here he blew out the twig from the fireplace he'd just used to light his pipe. "Not in the castle. Not in the stable nor on the grounds. Not in one a the prince's chambers."

"Ally!" admonished Deirdre.

"Just gone. Nobody knows why. And a'course once they were sure she weren't there and there'd be no more show-and-don't-tell for the gents, they most of them took off back home. But the really int'resting part I heard," he sat up self-importantly, "was that at least one of the princes left the castle before morning came, leaving the same night as Princess Lily. He knew somethin' the rest of 'em didn't. I'm just waiting to hear confirmation on whether they actually left together to steal out in the night, stealthy like."

"Hmm," Lily said thoughtfully, absorbing the news. "And have you heard which prince it was that did this sneaking out?"

"Yup. 'Twas Prince Salamander," said Alistair proudly.

"Alexander," corrected Deirdre.

"Right, Alexander," he nodded, "Prince of Sweethaven." Lily was beginning to think the two of them together might succeed as a gossip-hound, but apart they were puppies. "So if yer heading that way, fra Starling, you'll be gettin' all the news fra both sides."

"Indeed," said Lily with a little laugh. Her eyes were distinctly caramel now, and darkening to walnut by the minute. Both Deirdre and Alistair were looking at her, hungry, waiting for the next bit to add to their story. "Well, to be honest, I haven't heard that much more than you. Only that it has been suggested that this prince from Sweethaven was not a good man, and the princess didn't want to marry him." She just couldn't resist and was proud of herself for remembering to say "the princess" instead of "I".

Deirdre and Alistair looked at each other curiously. "But weren't there lots of princes to choose from? Why should she run off just because she didn't like one of 'em?" asked Deirdre.

Lily shrugged as nonchalantly as she could, she was just the messenger. "Maybe the king of Starling was gonna choose for her. Maybe she thought she had no choice." She leaned over her dinner bowl again, chasing one of the saved onions around the bowl with her fork.

"Huh," said both of them in polite dismay.

"Seems unlikely," said Deirdre. "King William is known fer 'is dislikke of fairies, but not for being cruel to his daughter.

She's mostly spoilt with magical trinkets and doted on, I hear."

"Besides," put in Alistair between smoky puffs, "we've met the prince as he was crossing this countryside and he's rather a nice fellow. Promised to speak with our duke about putting a library up for us common folk. More 'an likely she fell in love with him on the spot and they two run oft." Puff. "'Cept a'course they coulda just stayed and gotten married properly." Puff. "Naw, I can't make horns nor tails of it." Puff.

"Where'd you hear this wild theory anyway, dearie?" asked Deirdre.

Lily waved her hand in little circles, too many times, vaguely in the direction from which she'd come. "Oh, the cottage where I stayed last night. Probably just wild country gossip. Not like the kind you get here, in such a . . . well-traveled location."

Both innkeepers brightened at the flattery, forgiving her crazy theory from an ignorant cottar who probably didn't even read *The Knightly Times*.

Just then the door to the public room blew open with a great gust of wind, and a skinny, unkempt little man was blown in with it. He skidded a bit on the wooden floor and shoved his untidy brown hair out of his eyes, then closed the door and leaned against it a moment, as if to be sure wind wasn't going to fight back. Satisfied, he looked up at the occupants and smiled.

"Howdy, Deirdre. Alistair." After a moment when his eyes combed over Lily, he finished, "Miss."

"Why, Grady MacGinty, what're you doing so far afield of your pa's farm this time o' night?" asked Deirdre with welcome in her voice.

"I've started an adventure, Deirdre, as lotsa lads in these parts have," answered Grady, settling into a chair at the table, a short distance away from Lily. "A bunch of us heard 'bout Starling's bounty, and we're rousing to see if we can't get in on the action."

Alistair and Deirdre's eyes lit up at the mention of Starling, knowing this had to be a chapter in the tale that they had not yet heard. Lily's dark eyes grew round as well.

"Bounty?" said Alistair, unable to contain himself. "What's this abou' a bounty?"

"Well," said the young man slowly, enjoying the moment, "once the king heard his daughter was gone and realized she weren't comin' back on her own, he set round his grand hall with the fellas what had come to court his daughter."

Lily bit her tongue not to correct Grady about whether it was the Second Most Grand Hall, the Absolutely Most Grand Hall, or the Only Slightly Grand Hall for Barely Special Occasions.

"He'd conferred with his queen, and they decided the only way not to lose their heir and a chance fer her to marry was to set a bounty on her. King William said the first man to lay hands on her – not," he stopped and gestured to Lily, "in any crude way I don't mean, just find and get to where she is – should bring her back to Castle Starling, straight away. Then, the young man'd get five thousand gold pieces – that's right, *five thousand*," he said to Alistair and Deirdre's sighs of awe. "And, most importantly, he'd get the princess's hand in marriage." Grady sat up straight and smiled, then decided as an afterthought to thump the table for good measure.

The innkeepers oohed over this tasty bit of gossip. Deirdre even thumped Lily good naturedly on the shoulder, saying that it was a good thing her strange bit about Prince Alexander being unkind wasn't all they were left with.

After they quieted down, Lily managed to get out, "But the King promised whoever finds her will get to marry her, just like that? No questions asked?"

"Aye," said Grady seriously, though he couldn't stop himself smiling. "Not for nothing, mind you. He has to bring that ornery lady back to her father first, which I can't imagine will be an easy thing."

"No," agreed Alistair, "but what it'll be in the getting, ay, me boy!" He laughed heartily and slapped Grady's arm so hard the young man shuddered. "She's a right pretty wench, and with five thousand gold in yer pocket and a crown on yer head, you can forget about the rest you have to put up with!"

He and Grady roared with laughter. Deirdre frowned.

"Oh, that's enough, now," she said sternly. "It's not like *you* are gonna be chasin' her tail feathers, now are ye?" she said pointedly to her husband with some spite.

Alistair's laughter died and his posture crumpled.

"Well," he said with a sigh after a moment of silence, "you're sure it's anybody can get this bounty? Royalty's usually so particular 'bout who can marry whom. Why wouldn't he say 'twas only the princes and whatnot that was at her ball that could have her?"

"Oh no," Grady shook his shaggy head, "I heard it from Tom the milliner's boy, who got it from Reggie the tinker across the border, who heard it from a maid works up at the castle. Should be in next edition of *The Knightly Times*, you wait and see. It's anyone, which is why I'm here, heading back on the road she was s'posed to be running on, see if I can't catch her before those blokes from the castle meet up with her."

Lily was totally silent, staring at the table in front of her. She tuned out the men's conversation and thought about what she should do next. She decided it was a good thing they had stopped, or she never would have heard about the price on her head, or had it confirmed that her father would never let her choose her own husband.

Lily took the opportunity to say goodnight and excuse herself to her room upstairs, where her belongings and companions waited (save for Milwaukee, who was stabled), remembering at the last minute to take her leftovers with her. Deirdre promised to put a kettle on and bring water for washing as soon as it was hot.

The fairies came out of their hiding place when they heard Lily come in and drop onto the bed. Digging into the plate of pot roast, they asked her what was the matter.

"The word is out that I've run off and Prince Alex is apparently chasing after us. And my father offered a great sum of gold to any man who can catch me and take me back, where he will proceed to marry us on the spot," she summed up for them as she lay back with her arm thrown over her forehead in despair.

The fairies looked at one another as they chewed their dinner.

"And Deirdre's coming with a kettle so I can wash, so you'd better be prepared to hide again any minute."

Beloit chomped and swallowed. "Who's Deirdre?" he said, trying to change the subject.

Lily rubbed her hands up and down her face. "And they think I'm daft for running away just because I didn't like one prince. I mean I didn't tell them the whole thing about wing amputation and oubliettes and everything, but it sounded foolish the way they said it. 'Sounds unlikely,'" Lily said in an unkind imitation of Deirdre's voice. "I can't believe my father would do such a thing, let loose the dogs of wedding on my heels. It would be one thing if it was just the suitors – all fifty-nine of them, good goblins!" She stopped in her rant to pull at her long hair, twisting it in frustration. "But he said *any* man, of *any* class, who can kidnap and drag me back, gets to have me! It's even worse than I thought! At least if I had stayed and married Alexander, it would have been to a prince!" She took the tresses in her hands and buried her face in them, trying to hide from the horrible truth.

"That doesn' sound like something a king'd do," said Beloit tenderly. "Maybe that part o' the story is wrong."

Lily grabbed this gleam of hope in her mind, that maybe the roundabout way of country gossip had gotten it mixed up and confused. Before she could sort it out, there was a knock on the door. Deirdre, with the hot water.

"Who're you speaking to, dearie?" she asked, hauling in the kettle of steaming water and setting it by Lily's hearth.

"Oh, just mumbling to myself, I suppose," she said, waving her hand at the apparently empty room, the fairies having stowed themselves before Lily answered the door. "Just trying to work some things out, you know," she added with a faint smile.

"Sure," said Deirdre, as she finished pouring the water into the basin and laying out a clean cloth. When she turned back to Lily, a queer look came over her face.

"That's funny," she said. "Before by the fire downstairs, I thought that was a scar on your cheek, but here I see 'tis only a bit o' dirt." She reached up and plucked a crumb of dried clay off Lily's face and held it up as an example. "With that and the dust in your hair, 'tis no wonder you were so insistent on having hot water to wash."

Lily's courtly manners were under a great strain. Her eyes went positively mahogany. She looked at the bed behind her, and the large smudge of red dust where she had lain a moment ago. Taking one deep breath, she then turned back to the woman and said, "Yes, one can get so dirty on the road, without even noticing it." She let the rest of the measured breath out.

"Yes," said Deirdre, "one can." She tossed the crumb of dirt into the fire. "Well, I'll let you get on with it then. Good night."

"Good night," said Lily, closing the door again.

She was still leaning against the door listening when the fairies came out of the pack and looked at her with worry. She nodded when she could hear her hostess no longer.

"Do ya fink she's onto you?" asked Marzipan.

"I don't know," said Lily heavily. She walked over to the bowl of steaming water, dipped the cloth in and began scrubbing her face. "They seem to think something is up with me, Alistair thought it was strange for me to be traveling so far alone for instance, and now Deirdre knows I'm in disguise. That young man who told us about the bounty is still downstairs, but he doesn't seem any brighter than the innkeepers. I don't think they've actually put two and two together yet, or at any rate they can only get it to equal three. We have to get out of here, first thing tomorrow, crack of dawn and I mean it. I think we'll have to head into the woods straight-away, and skip through the wild lands to Hadesborough. The road's just not safe anymore."

Finished with her sponge-bath, she covered herself in a clean shift from her pack, setting out her hair brush and a magic firebrand on the small table as well. She took out her braids and brushed her long hair, sifting dust out of it with every stroke.

"Do you fink s'alright for us ta stay the night?" asked Beloit, worry raising his green eyebrows.

Lily softened when she looked at them. "We'll be fine, really. I think we're safe for now. We got a good head start on everyone but Alexander, and nobody's got a better horse than us, so we'll just go back to sleeping outside tomorrow night."

Beloit nodded, satisfied. "You're right about the horse," he said, as he and Marzipan resumed their dinner. "Prince Alexander 'asn't got a nicer one than Milwaukee." Marzipan nodded in agreement.

With a sigh as she finished, Lily sat down on the bed and said, "It feels so good to wash up for real. I can't wait till we get to the Castle Hadesburg and Queen Persephone." Pulling the coin purse off her dress, Lily dug her fingers into it. "The only advantage we have is that they don't know where we're going, only what direction." At last she pulled the ring out of the pouch and held it up between her forefinger and thumb. "That's what we'll do, find our own way till we're closer."

Slipping the ring onto her right ring finger, she held her hand out to look at it. *Worth a try anyway*, she thought. *Maybe the dragon will know something I don't.* Wishing the fairies a good night, she pulled the thick blankets over herself and blew out the candle.

Indeed the Ring of Green Dragon's Dreams was all that its name promised. Lily dreamed. . . .

I wake in the cave, in the quiet darkness, knowing the curves and crevices in it like I know my breath. At least it's dry in this one. No scale rot.

I stretch my long neck and feel the crinkle of the scales down my back and tail, shudder my wings a little. Was I this tired when I woke yesterday? Yesteryear? I am getting old, and for a dragon, that's saying something.

I blink in the twilight as I step into the open air, able to spread my wings in earnest. Cool tonight, and blue. Not quite raining, but seems to be thinking about it. Ah well, Maltese will not be happy. It's her birthday and this weather could ruin the birthday candles. Still, not quite raining.

I flap my wings, once, twice, trying them out. They seem strange to me all of a sudden, foreign. Was I dreaming of being a woman again? No, it's been years. I flap again hard and rise off the ground, my massive legs swaying. Now if I change shape, it takes a week to recover. No one would buy it anymore, not like when I was young, when I fell in love with my human, my Michael. So tender he was, and so strong. And so many years since he's visited my dreams. That must be it, why I feel so strange today. Hello, Michael, I've missed you.

I fly to the top of Mount Glorinn and settle on a rocky crag, waiting for the rest of the birthday party. I dream of the old days, when people were few and wild goats were plenty. I dream of flying over hills with the grace of an angel, the exuberance of youth.

Before long I spot Maltese, my red dragon friend, followed by Nuiin, the tiny golden dragon no bigger than a dog, and Carlyle, that old bronzey, who I've known for almost a millennium. They circle nearer, closing in on Mount Glorinn, and I rise to join them, the air mad with the beating of our wings. We blow the treetops double over with the beating of our wings. We make the mighty wind jealous with the beating of our wings and it pushes us higher above the mountain, buffeting us, carrying us. We circle like birds of prey, in mad glee at our freedom, a silent dragon greeting.

On the table, next to where the fairies slept, the cover of the Book of Enlightenment opened on its own.

One by one we taper off, led by the birthday girl, who rockets ahead to a farm a few miles off. Here we play our birthday game. We light the rail fenceposts on fire with a reckless sneeze, a pointed puff, a dangerous breath. The game is to see who can light the most posts on fire for her as others would blow candles out.

We don't hurt anyone, only eat one sheep or two, when the little boys are wading in the river, their crooks forgotten on the banks or dipped to steady a slippery foot on a slime-coated rock. They point and shout and call "Galoo!" to us in rapture.

Pages began to turn, fluttering faster, flipping faster, as the Book searched for something. The fairies stirred, turned in their sleep, but did not wake.

Carlyle seems to be lagging behind, so I slow down and let the others go on ahead as I turn to wait for him, hovering, seeing flashes of blue-green with every wingbeat. He looks even older than I remember when he catches up, then I realize it's been fifty years since our last meeting. He smiles a crookedy old dragon smile at me; bronzes are always charmers. "Why did we never mate?" he asks without preamble.

I smirk my green smile at him and turn a circle around him in the air. "Because you could never keep up with me!" I race forward towards where the others have gone.

The right page was open now, but no reader touched the Book, so its alarm grew stronger. The Book rose off the table, still showing the Right Page, and hovered before finding its direction. *There, on the bed, she's asleep.* Finding its reader at last, the Book floated across the room towards the dreaming princess.

Carlyle gives chase with a smokey laugh, rising higher to catch me, now turned upside down looking up at me from beneath as I look down on him. Then suddenly his crookedy smile goes flat, his face blank, and his wings miss their beat. He rotates in the air so he's facing down, away from me again, with what seems like impossible slowness. The bronze wings struggle to flap again, once, twice, then fail, and he plunges.

The others are far ahead now. I cry out, hoping at least they'll hear me and turn back, but Carlyle is falling fast and I dive toward him, arms outstretched. I grasp at his useless, trailing wings, ripping the membrane with a claw. I flap harder toward him, watch the ground come up, the world get bigger, we must be getting smaller – is it true dragons get smaller the closer they fly to the earth? – and finally get under him and my arms around his chest, but we're still falling. I can slow us down but we thump to the earth, bringing up a dust cloud in the field that swallows us.

While we are alone in the cloud, alone in the world for the moment, his head in my lap and my arms around his chest, he looks up at me and says, "I guess you were right. I couldn't." And he dies.

THUMP!

Lily woke as the Book landed next to her head on the bed and she sat violently upward, from the startlement of Book and Dream. She grabbed the magic firebrand on the bedside table and said "Alight!" to command its flame into being.

>HE'S HERE.

said the Book.

"Who's here?" said Lily.

>PRINCE ALEXANDER IS HERE.
>YOU MUST GO.
>NOW.
>GO.

"Is there . . . how far . . . but. . .can you tell me anything else?" she settled on finally.

>GO EAST.
>GO NOW.

Lily said a solemn thank you to her Book and threw the blankets off, leaping out of bed and setting the firebrand in a sconce on the wall. Dressing quickly, she was stuffing things back into her pack when the fairies awoke.

"Wos sat, then?" mumbled Beloit. "Somefing on fire??"

"We have to go, now. The Book woke me up," said Lily, not looking up from her packing. "He's coming."

Not bothering to ask who, the fairies roused themselves and packed as well, donning clean clothes and drinking clean water once more before leaving.

It wasn't long before the three of them were loaded with their packs and sneaking out into the hallway, firebrand in hand. The floorboards of the stairs creaked under their weight (or Lily's, anyway) but they were going too fast to look back to see if the innkeepers' door opened. Out the back door of the tavern, across the short yard to the stable, they saddled Milwaukee and strapped the bags on before you could say lemony snicket.

A light came on in an upstairs window as the trio rode around to the front of the inn. "I'll go up and see if I can spot 'em," offered Marzipan, flying off the horse and in the direction of Starling.

Before she returned, Lily herself could hear the hoofbeats, and considered a moment whether to go back around the building and hide till they had gone by, or ride out onto the road right away. Making up her mind, she kicked Milwaukee hard and leaned down, spurring him onto the road and southward, till they were around the next bend and she could take them safely off the road. Lily extinguished the firebrand with a word.

Waiting in the prickly darkness of the brush, they listened for the horses of their hunters to pass, but nothing came. After several minutes of stillness, Lily dismounted as quietly as she could, hoping they hadn't been spotted and tracked. She saw nothing on the road, and the only thing she heard was a sound that may have been an insect and may have been a bird, except for the fact that it was the wrong time of night for either to be awake and chirping. It sounded like this: "kennst-du-ingo". The sound came from somewhere above Lily's head.

Suddenly behind her, she heard an answering call: "ingo-ist-mein-freund." Then after a moment, Lily heard Beloit say, "It's Marzi trying to find us. Ingo-ist-mein-freund," he called again.

Lily returned to the horse as the strange fairy version of "marco polo" played out in the trees above her. When Lily had mounted Milwaukee again, Marzipan flew to her side and landed on the saddle next to her brother.

"They've gone into the inn," said Marzipan. "That's why they're not comin' down the road."

"That means they'll be talkin' to our charmin' hostess," put in Beloit.

"Well, can't be helped now," said Lily. "Are we all ready? We're going to head across country to the east, like the Book said."

When everyone was settled, Lily urged Milwaukee

through the trees and into the dark woods, were no paths seemed to go, without even a light to guide them.

Part Seven
In which Princess Lily Discusses Trolls, and
Attempts to Look Like One

I t was slow going through the woods that night. Fearing a torch would alert any trackers to their whereabouts, they had only the moonlight to see by, and the moon was only half full on the wax. The route they trod couldn't really be called a path. Perhaps at one time in a reckless moment a deer had wandered through here, but that was about as close as it got. To make things worse, the moon was the only fixed point they had to use for direction, and it set after a few hours. They had no idea whether their course had truly been east at all. When the moon was gone and it was still a few hours till dawn, Lily dismounted and had them rest again until the sun came up. Since they no longer traveled on the road, she decided the travel-only-at-night rule no longer applied.

The sun shone on a rather bedraggled crew that morning, for all their hearty meal and hot water luxury of the previous evening. As they once again ate a cold breakfast of fruit and bread, Lily consulted the Book for directions.

"We definitely need to head a little bit south today, if we want to have a straighter course," she said, "and a shorter one. This shows we did go a little out of the way last night, but I suppose since it was so slow going, it didn't really matter much."

And so they went south. Over the hills, south and east, until the trees got thicker and the hills more like plains. The Book indicated this was correct, that the straightest path to Hadesborough and Queen Persephone's court was through this forest, south and east. Lily continued to wear the ring when she slept at night, and continued to have visions through the eyes of an old female green dragon.

The first day out Lily was so concerned with putting

distance between herself and the inn that she spared a thought for nothing else. It was easier that way, not thinking of the twisted sense of propriety of her father, nor the nasty and dull and insipid men that had attended her gala who might be chasing her, nor the disgusting prospect that someone like Grady MacGinty would be the one to capture her in the end. Most awful of all, she could not bear to think of the cruel and despicable Prince Alexander who was most definitely on her heels.

On the second morning in the forest, she realized it was foolish to avoid the truth. She had to decide what to do next. If she believed what Grady had said about the bounty, then it surely would be reported in the gossip columns within the week. Would *The Knightly Times* run an image of Princess Lily with the story? Castle Starling boasted a gallery of royal family portraits, but the traveling painter had not returned to the kingdom for two years, so Lily's last portrait was woefully out of date. Or perhaps gleefully so. Even if they could get the royal painting and publish it, it wouldn't look exactly as Lily did now. At least she would have some leverage with her disguise.

It was a sunny afternoon and the princess was leading the horse through a particularly rocky bit of woods. The fairies, who had been some help navigating with their eye-in-the-sky technique that they had used on the road, were giving it a rest and basking in the sunlight from a perch on the saddlebags. They didn't seem to notice Lily slowing the pace of the horse, as she cast about in the foliage of the forest floor, looking for something.

"Naw, I'd have ta say they're not my favorite," said Beloit, continuing his story. "Trolls can run a good game o' poker, but all too often it turns into a game of poke her, poke him, poke the dog. And if you ever do play cards wiv trolls, don't let them deal."

"Are they cheaters?" asked Lily, poking with the toe of her boot around a clump of mushrooms at some ferny looking plants.

"Naw," said Beloit, "they just make the cards sticky."

"Very messy creatures, trolls," agreed Marzipan, who lay back with her hands behind her head and her eyes closed.

"I've never actually met any trolls," said Lily, examining an oblong leaf she had picked up, "only read about them. There's a lot of things I've only read about." She sighed and dropped the leaf behind her.

"Wot you soundin' sad about it for?" asked Marzipan, turning her head and opening her purple eyes to look at Lily. "You're out 'ere, in the wild, havin' adventures. Not stuck up in that tower, wiv only your book to entertain you." She closed her eyes again and lay back.

"I know," said Lily, who didn't sound the least convinced. "I guess I thought adventuring would be more, I dunno, adventurous or something. Not like the challenge of finding a place to sleep that's not muddy or having to brush your horse every day. No offense," she added for Milwaukee's benefit and patted him on the nose. "I just thought maybe I could see some more things I'd read about, not just more trees."

"You're saying it isn't entertaining enough for you to be runnin' fer your life from an evil prince, eh?" said Beloit. "That a little bit too ord'nary?" He grinned, feeling clever.

"Of course that's not what I mean. I just would think it was very interesting to play poker with trolls, for instance." She stopped Milwaukee in his tracks, let go of the reins, and bent over to investigate a bit of shrubbery.

Beloit stood up on his saddlebag and put his hands to his hips. He took a big breath and said, "Qu- what are you doing?" He deflated in his confusion.

"Looking for wartberries," replied Lily, not looking up from her botany. "I'm highly allergic. They make me turn a blotchy red, and little hard cysts to form under the skin anywhere it touches me. And if I swallow it, . . . well," she trailed off, as if finishing that sentence was too horrific to contemplate.

Beloit shook his head, hands still braced on his hips, and looked incredulously at his lazing sister, who had opened her eyes. "Are we not givin' her enough attention, d'ya think? She's the only human around fer miles that we could play servants to, and she's gotta make herself into a wart-faced hag to get some sympathy?"

"It's not for you that I'm doing it," Lily said. She duck-walked over to the next shrub and began pulling leaves off of it. She gave a little "ha" of triumph.

Lily took a moment to cast a reproachful look in Beloit's direction. "It's not as if the two of you have been doing much in the way of serving, lately." Beloit huffed and sputtered, but Marzipan shrugged and closed her eyes again.

"So why the hag face, then?" Marzipan asked.

"For a disguise." She gathered a handful of marble-sized berries, knobbly-surfaced and grubby brown with bright red stems, into the hem of her skirt, careful not to touch them with her bare fingers. "I haven't wanted to scare you, but I am really worried about all those men who are supposedly chasing us. Well, chasing *me*," she corrected. "There's no telling how many are out there looking for me, and I think we're pretty safe for now, away from other people as we are in the forest."

She shooed Milwaukee back a few steps as she sat cross-legged and picked up two nearby stones to make a mortar and pestle. "Before long, though, we're gonna be in Castle Hadesburg with people who will surely have heard about the bounty, and possibly have a good idea what I look like."

She rolled a few berries off her skirt onto the larger rock, then trapped them with the other, and pressed down so that a thin stream of snot-like ooze drooled out between the rocks.

Grimacing slightly, Lily went on. "I've been trying to think of something to change the way I look. The dust in the hair and the fake scar were really temporary. They didn't even hold up for one night."

"Yeah, 'specially after yer tantrum. You need somefing sturdier," agreed Beloit, and instantly looked sheepish when Lily's dark look bored into him.

"So," she continued, teeth slightly clenched, "I thought about cutting my hair, but, but, I thought if I could avoid that it would be easier to tease or braid or something," she finished quickly. I'm sure you don't need me to tell you that a princess as beautiful as Lily could not help being a bit attached to her good looks. It was a wonder she was willing to give up her lovely complexion on her face, even temporarily.

"The wartberries will make my face look strange, but it doesn't really hurt or itch, so long as I can keep from picking at it. I had my first run-in with wartberry as a child. I'd fallen off my horse into a patch of it. My face and neck and all down my left side puffed up and changed color when I was about ten. Martha put me to bed for a day and a night and made me drink rose-leaf tea, and it cleared up in no time."

Lily picked up a large maple leaf and wiped the brown wartberry ooze onto it. With a look of disgust mingled with determination, she shut her eyes tight and wiped the gunk onto her right jawbone and down to her chin. She repeated the process, crushing more berries, gathering the ooze on the leaf, and applying it to her face, until she had doused her forehead, her right eyebrow, and her collarbone. Luckily the odor was faint and herbal. She got a handkerchief from the saddlebags and picked as many more wartberries as she could fit into the cloth when she tied the corners together to make a ball. "For later, when this batch wears off," she said to the grimacing fairies.

They walked on. After about half an hour, Lily could stand it no longer. She doused a cloth in water from her flask and wiped the now-dried wartberry ooze off her face. The fairies admired the effect, telling her how one eyebrow seemed to have grown down to meet her cheekbone, her forehead was a rippling Cro-Magnon masterpiece, and the blotchy patches of red splashed across her collarbone looked a little bit like their mother. Lily was laughing and nodding under the washcloth when a noise out of the quiet forest startled her.

Suddenly there was a crash in the bush right in front of the horse, as something large and clumsy fell off a small rocky precipice to their right. Lily and Milwaukee took a few hurried steps back as the bush seemed to move and writhe on its own, wiggling its tiny green leaves higgledy-piggledy. A flash of blue where it shouldn't be rose up from the bush, and a hand appeared on the end of it. This hand and blue-clad arm wrestled with the bush till its mate was unsnared as well, this second hand clutching a sword.

At last the hands seemed to get a grip on their owner and pull him from the wreckage of the bush, so that before them stood a young man with blond hair to his shoulders wearing a blue tunic, shaking leaves off himself and picking twigs off his clothing as if he were a wet, twig-ridden dog.

He held his sword up at a slight angle, not quite high enough to be menacing, but not entirely forgotten.

"Are you alright?" asked Lily finally, as the young man continued with his grooming without speaking.

"Hm?" he said, looking up as he found a particularly stubborn stick in his hair and pulled it so the blond tress stood up off his head.

"I said, are you alright?" said Lily again. "You took quite a fall, I think," she said unsurely, realizing she wasn't entirely sure where he'd come from.

"Oh, hm, yes," he mumbled, turning around and pointing at the precipice vaguely with his sword. "I really ought to be more careful. That's the third time this week."

He continued to drag at the stick in his hair.

Lily waited.

Marzipan and Beloit floated up off the saddlebags to get a better look at the stranger.

The strange young man finally dislodged the stick and held it, with the serious chunk of blond hair that had come with it, triumphantly up in front of him. He then looked from the stick to the princess with a faint smile, as if expecting her to congratulate him.

"So, . . . do you live around here?" asked Lily finally, leaning forward.

The man looked from the hairy twig in his hand to the sword in his other hand and said "oh" as if startled. "Yes, I remember now. Ahem.

"Halt!" he said in an entirely different and rather

pompous voice, holding up his sword toward them eagerly. "You are entering the realm of Jonquilline, the great and terrible green dragon of Glorrin. You must stop, and pay homage, and make her some tea, and spread butter on her biscuits, and trim her nails, and tell her she looks terrific in that particular shade of green," he took a deep breath in order to continue, "and sweep out her cave, and fetch her some strawberries (unless strawberries are out of season or already completely picked by the previous homage-payers in her realm, in which case she will take bosc pears instead), and . . . and . . . ." He stopped. His sword drooped. "And!" The sword rose again. "And pay her homage, or you shall leave this realm, now and forever forthwith." He smiled at the trio, who said nothing. "Amen," he added, signaling he was done by twirling the sword in little circles.

After a long pause, "I'd take that as a yes," said Beloit.

"Ah," started Lily, "so, we're in the realm of a green dragon, you say?"

"Indeed, madam. And sir," he said to Beloit, "and madam," to Marzipan.

"And you are her. . . gatekeeper?" suggested Lily.

The young man brightened at this. "Gatekeeper," he said and nodded. "A title. Ooh, I *like* that," he said with relish.

"Are you really banishin' us from the dragon's realm?" asked Marzipan irreverently. "And all that whosie-wotsis about strawberries, you 'spect us to believe that?"

"Well, you must pay homage if you want to avoid banishment," he said. "There's no question of that. And Jonquilline does enjoy her spot of tea when she has company. But the strawberries," he shrugged, "the strawberries are for me. She'd rather have bats as a garnish than strawberries any day."

"All right, then," said Lily. "I expect we can work out a suitable arrangement with her. Take us to the dragon."

Blond eyebrows shot up toward the still-leafy blond hair. "Beg pardon?"

"Take us to your liege. The dragon," said Lily slowly. "Jonquilline of Glorrin?"

"To pay homage and all that," added Beloit with a smirk.

"You can't be serious," said the young man earnestly. "You can't mean that you want to see the great and terrible Jonquilline. I mean it's just not done." He crossed his arms belligerently in front of his chest, which was very awkward considering the adjustments he had to make because of the sword.

"Wotchu mean, 'it's not done'?" asked Marzipan in disbelief. "You just made a whole speech about tea and butter and shades of green, and you clearly didn't make that up on the spot, love, so why'd you memorize that whole thing if we can't see the dragon?"

"Well, it's just, it's not that you can't see her," he said. "It's just that it's not done, that's all. Nobody's ever asked before. They always just go away. The bit about trimming a dragon's nails and strawberrying is intimidating, you know." He looked at Lily for support.

"Well, I'm not intimidated," replied the princess. She turned to her companions. "Are you intimidated, Beloit?"

"Not in the least," he assured her with a nod of his green head.

"Marzipan?"

"Tcha" was all she said, hovering over the horse with her arms crossed.

"It's settled then," she said, turning back to the young man. "We want to see this dragon."

The young man gulped, almost audibly. "You're sure you wouldn't rather go strawberrying?"

"We're sure," replied Lily sternly.

The young man started stomping through the undergrowth toward the precipice from which he had fallen. His path slowly drifted to the left, and before long the companions saw that there was an easy slope behind the precipice with a well-trammeled trail. Up this they walked, the path wide enough even for Milwaukee to make it with no trouble. They made their twisting way through the woods, down the path that had obviously been made by the young man's frequent comings and goings. He stomped along ahead of them, silent and seeming glum.

After a few minutes, they came to a clearing rimmed with birch trees and filled like a pool with waves of tall grass. Great boulders littered the ground and stuck up through the underbrush of the trees, like discarded pocket lint from a giant that had been petrified. A knoll on the other side of the clearing was covered in summer strawberries. A great pomegranate tree stood up in the middle of them, like a man on stilts in a crowd.

As they approached this knoll, Lily could see a shadow in its side, a dark maw yawning at the sun. A cave, she realized. More than that, a cave she had seen in her dream. Her surroundings were suddenly, shockingly familiar: the birchwood circle, the waves of grass, the tall red man standing over the hill. She knew before they got close enough to hear it that there was a spring on the north side of the entrance to the cave. They were about to meet the dragon she dreamed she had been when she slept wearing the magic ring.

"A spring!" cried Beloit in some excitement. "I've been drinkin' from a canteen for days! Finally fresh water!" Without waiting to be invited, he dashed forward in flight to land on the rocky edge of the spring's pool.

"Would it be alright if we had some water from your spring?" asked Lily in all politeness, even though Beloit was already dipping both hands in and scooping water up to his open mouth. "Perhaps we could fill our canteens, and let our horse drink?"

"Well, I don't know, I mean Jonquilline might not like fairies bathing in her spring. . . ." said the young man.

"I'm only drinkin'," protested Beloit between slurps.

"And the horse – that is, he's a lovely beastie, but I just don't know what she'll do. Maybe have you all for a barbecue, in which case you won't be thirsty any more."

"Why not?" asked Marzipan.

"Because you'll be grilled over an open dragon's mouth,"

he said shortly.

"You really don't 'ave this 'intimidate the tourists' bit down, love. It just doesn't suit you," said Marzipan with a sigh. "You can't pull off a 'be afraid, very afraid' shtick. Maybe you ought to work on yer act." She flew over to the pool and joined her brother.

"Yeh," said Beloit, sitting back on his heels, thirst sated. "We don't even know fer sure there's a dragon hereabouts anyways."

"Oh, there's a dragon alright," said Lily and the young man together. For the first time, they laughed together.

"And I did not say you could drink from my spring, Soula-Mays!" said a voice from the darkness of the cave, a voice like a river, or a fire, smooth at its center and sharply crackling at its edges, with deep melodic undertones.

Beloit and Marzipan shot into the air and several feet away from the cave mouth into the clearing. Lily, unmoving, peered into the cave and saw a glint off two shiny spots that she realized after a moment must be the dragon's eyes. A row of ivory teeth, aged and very large, curled up in a strange grin in the dim entrance.

Part Eight
In which Enters a Dragon

The dragon moved slowly, listing from side to side as she moved her feet forward in her own time, blinking as if she had just woken from a nap. As she approached the mouth of the cave, Lily began to make out her shape. Triangular head with bony protrusions on the back. Long, thick, almost graceful neck. Legs tapered, rippled with muscle, but almost dainty in their slenderness.

Jonquilline stepped the front half of her body into the light and everyone could see she had a genuine smile on her wide, emerald green face. The fairies kept their distance, and it was a moment before Lily heard the low rumbling that flowed and rolled and got louder and wider as the dragon lifted her head and laughed. The fairies didn't seem to think this improved their situation greatly, but Lily was not afraid.

"It was worth it just to see you move so fast," the dragon said, still laughing like a waterfall. "Fwoosh!" she said, imitating their flight by waving one elegant green hand.

"I tried to stop them, your most grand and reticent Majesty," said the young man. "I warned them about the consequences, of the homage they must pay to your gratuitousness, and they said they wanted to see you to arrange it."

"Oh, not the bit about the strawberries *again*," said the dragon, shaking her massive head to one side in reproof.

"Well, at least I remembered to take my sword, your grandioseness." He held it up at a non-threatening height as evidence.

"And did you fall off the precipice again?" asked the dragon. When he didn't answer, she said, "That's the third time this week. You know our supply of wool for mending your tunic isn't going to last forever." She sighed, sounding for all the world like an overworked housewife. "And stop it with those ridiculous titles. You know I'm not the queen or high commander of anything"

"I couldn't help it, Jonny!" he whined. "They weren't following the path at all, so none of my alarms sounded, so I jumped up from where I lay on the hill with my sword raised and my speech ready and I just went too far, over the edge instead of on it, that's all." It was his turn to sigh, frowning and slapping the flat of his sword on his knee.

The dragon turned from him to face Lily. "You'll have to excuse Sir Aaron. He's . . . you'll just have to excuse him. He's harmless, really. The only one he's ever hurt is himself."

She stepped slowly out of the cave, shoulders coming into the sunlight, revealing the ribbed wings folded together over her spine like a Chinese fan. Lily could just see a little of the bluish membrane peeking out. Her long serpentine body followed, and followed, and finally tapered over thick back legs into a tail.

The most amazing thing about seeing a green dragon in full daylight, as you may know from your own adventures, was the colors of her scales that covered all her body. They weren't just one green but a whole array of green hues, darker around the features of her face, her eyes and lips and nostrils, almost a forest green, and the rest of her face a translucent emerald. Her wings were outlined in an aqua green, her legs and body fading from a bright hue to a dusky one from her backbone to her toes. All of her scales seemed dusted in an opaline powder, making them sparkle and shine.

They could only tell she was an older dragon by the sag in the loose flesh on her chest and along her belly, and by the tiny spots around her eyes and lips that had lost all color, flecking her with white.

"I am Jonquilline, of Glorrin," said the dragon in her deep, rippling voice.

"I know," said Lily softly.

"And I presume my resident knight, Aaron, has already introduced himself," she said, pointing to the blond man in blue.

Aaron looked up at Lily, picking under his nails with the tip of his sword.

"We actually weren't properly introduced," said Lily. "I'm prrrvilet," she said, remembering at the last moment who she wasn't supposed to be.

"Pervilet," said the dragon, trying it out. "That's . . . unusual."

"Well, I generally just go by 'Violet,'" the princess said finally, able to think of nothing else but her second middle name. "And that's Beloit, and the other one is Marzipan." She gestured over her shoulder and turned to the clearing where the fairies had gone. At Lily's introduction, they flew closer slowly, Marzipan in the lead.

Jonquilline turned her green head to one side as she looked at them, the sun glinting off the blue spikes that rose from the back of her skull. "Hello," she said in her fiery, watery voice.

Marzipan stopped and floated mid-air in front of her, arms crossed. Beloit hovered behind and slightly above, peeking over her shoulder. After a few moments of staring, Marzipan spoke.

"How did you know we were Soula-Mays?" she asked suspiciously.

Jonquilline closed her eyes and brought her head back up to neutral. "Oh, dragons know a lot of things," was all she said, and opened her black eyes again, looking at Marzipan.

"That's it?" She shrugged her tiny shoulders, making her overalls bounce. "You know a lot o' things? Out 'ere, middla nowhere, with your knight errant falling off cliffs and goin' on 'bout strawberrying, an' you just guess our tribe?"

Jonquilline squinted a bit and frowned. "Soula-Mays have quite a reputation in these woods. You're impertinence at the spring gave you away. Besides," added Jonquilline with a haughty sniff, "your accent is unmistakable."

"Tcha," said Marzipan in poorly feigned disbelief.

"Wot accent?" grumbled Beloit. "We're not ta ones wot talks funny." He crossed his arms across his chest and looked away, a mirror image of his sister's pose.

"I thought the Soula-Mays lived east of here, between Hadesborough and Sweethaven," said Lily.

"They do," answered Jonquilline, "but it's all part of the same forest. And though I call this cave and meadow my home, I am a frequent flyer, you see," she said, flapping her blue-green wings ever so slightly.

"Of course," said Lily with smile, remembering flying in her dreams and shrugging her shoulders under her shirt a little.

Milwaukee, understanding none of the etiquette involved in drinking from other people's springs, began to move forward and tug on the reins in Lily's hand. "Would you mind terribly if my horse had a drink? He's been drinking out of a canteen, like the rest of us, for days." She dug her heels in and strained against the reins, determined not to let him go till it was deemed polite.

"By all means," answered the dragon graciously. "You are welcome to it, but perhaps you'd rather let your horse drink at the stream." She pointed at the rivulet formed by the runoff that ran around the base of the hill. "His standards of water purity are not as high as yours, I expect. And you, too, Marzipan, Beloit, you may drink your fill." When they remained at a distance with their tiny arms crossed, she surrendered a smile. "Honestly, I was only having a bit of fun. Do let's get on and be friends."

Her reptilian smile must have been too much for them – she seemed so greenly sincere – because slowly they uncrossed their arms and flew over to the spring.

Lily suppressed a little gasp as she caught her reflection in the clear pool. The effect of the wartberries, now a few hours old, was quite remarkable. Lily wondered with horror what part of the red rash on her chest resembled the fairies' mother.

Once everyone had drunk at the spring, the princess, the fairies, the dragon and the knight sat on the grass in front of the dragon's cave and had a tea party, consisting of the peppermint leaf tea the knight had made, as well as some strawberries and pomegranates collected from the hill. Lily promised to use her bow to bring back some game from the forest later.

"So, Aaron said you usually banish people who come into your realm and wouldn't see them," started Lily. "Does that happen often? Is it to keep away your enemies?"

"Oh, the banishment speech was Aaron's idea," said Jonquilline, looking at her blond knight fondly. "I'm really too old to have many enemies left. But we still do get the occasional prince or lad trying to impress a lass who comes looking to slay a dragon. Aaron here is my bodyguard, so to speak."

Aaron smiled. "That's what Miss Perviolet said, she said I was a keepgater, like it was a title."

"You can have a title if you want," said Jonquilline.

"So if knights gen'rally come ta slay you," said Beloit, "how'd you end up wiv this fellow guarding you?"

"Have you ever tried to slay a dragon?" asked Aaron. "It's bloody hard."

"Yes, it is," agreed Jonquilline with a laugh. "Once a dragon reaches a certain age, lives through a certain number of assassination attempts, she's learned enough tricks to stay alive, and get the knights to lose interest in the quest. So that way she doesn't have to actually kill the knights any more, roast them or eat them or what have you." She lifted a clawed foot and inspected it closely, as if reminiscing.

"You know how to toy with them enough so they feel like they tried hard, but let them know they should go home after a while. This one," she sighed, "didn't seem to want to go home."

"Maybe he jus' couldn't take a hint," muttered Marzipan. Beloit snickered.

Ignoring this, Jonquilline went on. "He stayed so long trying to slay me that I started to get rather used to him, and finally I asked him to stay and work as my bodyguard, to keep other slayers away."

"Good job it is, too, Jonny," said Aaron. "Lotsa strawberries. And I get to wield my sword," he added gladly.

"Wot kinda health benefits d'you get wiv it?" inquired Beloit.

"Apothecary, chirurgeon, and wisewoman at a 20 per cent

co-pay," replied Aaron.

Beloit nodded, impressed. "D'you get herbalist, or has it gotta be the wisewoman on your plan? Workin' at Castle Sweethaven, we got –"

"So you two became companions," interrupted Lily, cutting Beloit off, "instead of enemies. What a fascinating story!" She exaggerated just how interested she was to cover up the blush that rose in her face at the mention of Sweethaven.

"Exactly," said Jonquilline. "He keeps a watch, I guard the cave and keep it warm, he hunts the game and I roast it for us. Keeps us both entertained."

"Indeed," said Lily with approval.

"So, you haven't told us your story yet. What are two Soula-Mays and a young woman doing crossing through the great forest by themselves?" asked the dragon.

There was a short silence as Lily, Marzipan and Beloit exchanged looks of deliberation. After the trouble her lies had caused at the inn, Lily thought it best to stick as close to the truth as possible.

"We're heading to the Castle Hadesburg. We heard Queen Persephone runs a halfway castle for girls and that's why I'm going," said Lily.

"I see," said Jonquilline. "And the Soula-Mays, are they going home or going to the halfway castle with you?" She turned her large, shiny obsidian eyes on Marzipan and Beloit.

"Oh, well, um," said Lily.

"We're her servants," said Marzipan quickly. "We go where she goes. She don't know yet if we'll get to go home."

"Interesting," said Jonquilline under her breath.

Turning back to the princess after a moment, the dragon said, "There's no road that goes through the forest to Hadesborough, do you know that? There's the river, that runs roughly east and west, through Soula-May territory before it connects up with a road to Castle Hadesburg. It's quite a bit south of here, though, and I don't know how far that steed of yours will make in the thick woods to the south. Is there. . . something you wish to avoid, that's making you take such a round-about way?"

Lily paused, but again decided to stick to the truth. "My father was going to make me marry somebody I couldn't live with. That's why I had to run away. I'm hoping Queen Persephone can take me in and help me find a place to go next."

"I see," said Jonquilline. She seemed to sense this was the end of the story, as she turned to Aaron and asked for more tea, and they resumed their party until night fell.

Over the next few days the princess and the fairies grew comfortable with their new friends and their home in meadow, cave, and hill. The strawberries were in season, the grass was soft, the water at the spring was sweet. Even the wild animals of the woods cooperated by falling under Lily's arrows, providing plenty of meat for everybody.

One afternoon the two humans went out in the area surrounding the cave so Aaron could complete his patrol, and so Lily could hunt for game with her bow and arrows. Aaron was making her lie down for the fifth time as he crawled on his belly behind a hedge. She was really getting tired of it, and her blistering face was beginning to itch from all the dirt. She realized as she patted her face gingerly, trying not to pick at the lumps, that she would have to make another application of wartberry that day. The results of the first one were beginning to fade.

There had been no sign of any passerby larger than a tree squirrel at any of Aaron's checkpoints. After five minutes of waiting quietly, Lily said again, "Aaron, this is useless."

"Shht! I can hear something rumbling, like hoofbeats or something." He continued to peek out at the clearing as he put his ear to the ground. "There it is again."

"Yes, that's my stomach," replied Lily dryly. "We're overdue to catch something for lunch. I'm starving."

"Just a few moments more, I really think I hear someone coming," he insisted.

With a heavy sigh, Lily heaved herself up onto her arms and began to get up. "Well, you can play guard dog all you like, but I'm going to play hunter –"

She stopped as she heard voices from the trees on the other side of the clearing. At the same moment, Aaron grabbed her wrist and pulled her down again.

"I don't see how ya know where yer goin'," said a man's voice full of bitterness. "I've 'ad just about enough of your ideas o' trackin'."

"My dear barbarian, if you would shut your hairy mouth for more than two minutes, you might observe, and learn," said a somewhat higher male voice in response. "I've been telling you, I'm quite sure she came into the woods after leaving the inn. I saw the horse tracks going off the road."

"Doesn' mean 'twas her horse. Coulda been anyone wiv a horse," argued the first man.

"And did you happen to note that not twelve hours prior to our lady taking residence at said inn, that the area experienced a torrential downpour? Anyone else's hoofprints would have been washed away, forthwith," insisted the second in nasally tones.

Lily began to tremble where she lay. She still couldn't see the speakers, though the noise of their approach was getting louder. Neither did she recognize the voices right off, but by their comments she instantly knew they were following her own trail from Alistair and Deirdre's pub. Aaron lay next to her, still holding her wrist and staring out through the bushes for sight of the intruders. She grabbed his hand in her own, trying to think of what to do.

"And jus' why would such a royal miss wanta go into the woods, anyway? There're no shoemakers or milliners in here, no fancy dress parties, no chefs fer cookin' up a feast. Why wouldn't she stay on the road?"

A great sigh of exasperation sounded and there was a noise of branches being shoved roughly aside. "Because, my poor troglodyte, she is running away. She doesn't want to be found. I sincerely hope she brought an assortment of footwear when she packed, so that she might be properly attired for such a journey. Perhaps there are no fancy dress parties here but there are any number of opportunities for enlightenment and exercise."

Lily groaned inwardly as she recognized the voice from this last comment. It was Prince Carlton Shelton Lewiston Worthington of East Cloudland, who had an abominable hunting obsession, as well as what Lily considered an alarming concern for proper clothing. He had talked her ear off about his hunting conquests and gave detailed descriptions of his outfits for each before her father had rescued her and shuttled her on to the next audition. I mean, introduction.

Branches parted to reveal several men entering the east side of the clearing from where Lily and Aaron hid. The man in front was slight and short, brown hair curling to almost ludicrous proportions, wearing a bright red beret perched on top of his afro. His coat had wide vertical stripes in Blue, Red, and Green, with smaller accent stripes of Gold in between. (The colors were gaudy enough to warrant Capital Letters.) This ostentatious gentlemen was followed by a broad, tall fellow with dark brown hair and a long, scruffy red beard. Clearly, by the way his head bent toward Prince Carlton, this was the other speaker. Behind them came two younger men, probably squires, leading several horses.

When the troupe came fully into view, Lily felt Aaron gearing up to charge, his muscles tensing under her hand. She clutched his arm and bent close to him.

"Leave them, Aaron!" she whispered urgently. "They're passing through. We can just wait for them to pass!"

Aaron's blond head swung around at her and stared in astonishment. "Perviolet, surely you don't expect me to sit here while strangers tramp through Jonny's realm without so much as a 'where's your lunch bucket?' What kind of a keepgrater would I be if I did that?"

"No, Aaron, please!" she cried in terror, as loud as she dared. "They're almost gone!"

He turned back to the clearing and saw the gaudy man's retreating back as he turned down another supposed path. "I'd better hurry up, then."

Sliding through Lily's grasping hands, he stood and leapt over the bush, stopping a few feet from the slope. Lily sighed very quietly in thanks that he had not tumbled this time.

"Halt!" he cried, raising his sword at the strangers, who immediately turned around. "I hereby banish you from the realm of Jonquilline, the green dragon of Glorrin, whose dirt you now trod and whose pansies I see you have trampled. You must stop, and pay homage, and make her some tea, and pick her some strawberries . . . etcetera, and so forth, Bob's your uncle, . . . or you will be banished from her realm, now and forever. Amen."

The strangers looked at each other as if confirming they had all seen the same thing. After a bit of nodding and grunting, the red bearded man addressed the knight.

"Oi," he said. "Did you just banish us, then tell us to make tea, then banish us again?"

"What?" said Aaron. "I . . . no, I said, let me see. I said you are in the realm of the green dragon," he counted on his fingers, "then that you have to pay homage," a second finger, "then I said that if you *don't* pay homage you'll be banished. Yes, that's it." He held up his three fingers as evidence.

"Right," agreed Red Beard. "But when you first said we was in the green dragon's realm, you said we was banished from it."

Aaron scratched his head with his three counting fingers. "Did I?" He swung his sword around a couple times, taking practice swings like a baseball player. "Yeah, I guess I did. Huh. I guess you're banished then."

"Excuse me," Prince Carlton interrupted and stepped forward. "Can you tell me, have you seen anyone pass this way in the last couple of days?"

"This way?" started Aaron, making Lily's heart jump. "No, not this way. You're the only ones've tramped this trail since late winter. See how you trampled those posies?" He pointed with his sword at a crushed plant with purple flowers. "Those are new this year. No one's come this way at all."

"I see," the short prince said with extreme patience. "What

of the rest of the forest in this vicinity? Anyone traveling other roads through the forest?" His bushy eyebrows rose as if talking to a demented four-year-old.

Aaron laughed at this. "There's no road through this forest, sir. Only roads are what we make, me and the dragon. O' course she flies mostly, so her roads are different than mine. Up in the air." He pointed his sword-tip at the sky in all seriousness.

A bizarre smirk was erupting on Prince Carlton's face. He seemed unfavorably amused at Aaron's speech. "I see. This dragon of which you speak. She's your friend, I suppose? Have you ever in all your loud years heard of a dragon and a knight being friends, Burly?" he asked his bearded comrade.

Burly smiled through his hair now, too. "Sure haven't, yer highness."

"Is she up there right now, sir knight? Doing loop-de-loops above your head?" Prince Carlton's already nasally voice rose to an shrill quiver in his mockery.

"Of course not," answered Aaron, bewildered. "I can't see her, anyway," he revised, looking up. "I suppose she could be anywhere at the moment."

The strangers were chuckling in earnest now. Prince Carlton even pointed at Aaron as he laughed and looked at his companions. "No doubt, next you'll be regaling us with a tale of dining with fairies and say you have Princess Lily hiding behind one of these bushes."

He pointed directly at the bush from which Aaron had sprung, where Lily remained lying on the ground. She wanted to creep farther into the shadows but didn't dare move lest she be seen.

"Who?" said Aaron.

"Princess. Lily," said Prince Carlton with exaggerated slowness. "Good goblins, don't you read The Knightly Times? What kind of a knight are you, haha?" He turned and exchanged another guffaw with his men. "Princess Lily of Starling has run away, and I am going to find her."

Burly mumbled something insistently, cutting Prince

Carlton off.

"Yes, yes, that is, *we* are looking for her," he amended with a roll of his squinty eyes, "and whichever one of us finds her, will take her to wife. If you weren't such a buffoon, you could even share in the reward and help us look."

"Why would a princess marry you just because you found her in some woods?" asked Aaron.

Prince Carlton gave a growl and tugged in mock exasperation at his hair, then seemed to recall himself and straightened his beret before continuing.

"King William of Starling has offered gold to any man who can find her and bring her back. Any man –" he hastened to add, "who attended her gala and was already approved to court her, that is. Which excludes *you*." His thin lips curled in an ugly sneer at Aaron. "He'll get a sum of gold and he'll get the lady's hand, and I am anxious to get on with it, so you had better let us get on our way." He finished with a twirl of his hand in dismissal and turned on his heel, intending to stomp off. He was prevented by the complete lack of clear path in front of him, and he looked around, confused.

"Hang on!" protested Aaron, walking down the slope a few feet. "You can't just go on plodding through the forest when you've been banished!"

"Oh yeah?" said Prince Carlton, turning back around and swaying with bravado. "Well, I would be more than happy to get on our way if you would stop yammering at us, you officious little lap-dog."

"Well, that's . . . good," concluded Aaron. "I'll lead you out, see that you don't cross the stream and enter our realm. You'll be successfully banished, then." He nodded, satisfied with the plan.

Prince Carlton made an exaggerated bow to Aaron, sweeping his beret off his head, and replacing it with care when he stood up again. "My gratitude for your blundering acceptance of my wish to depart is paramount, Sir Left Foot."

He threw his arms out in a gesture of "Lead on!" to Aaron,

waiting for the knight to descend the slope. Lily held her breath as she waited to hear whether Aaron would go on without her, or call back and show them all that Princess Lily of Starling, most highly prized runaway in the Enlightened Kingdoms, lay wart-faced in the dirt.

Part Nine
In which An Invitation Arrives Just In Time

For one horrible moment, Lily thought Aaron would remember her lying behind the bush and call back, but after a slight hesitation, he marched down to the front of the troupe of men who were searching for her. Prince Carlton the Fop followed in a sweep of color, Burly and the squires giggling as they brought up the rear.

Lily lay on the ground, making herself one with the dirt, caring no longer that her face itched and her frock was soiled. Her hands trembled as she hugged her arms around her chest. Her heart was booming like a fireworks display. She felt cold all over, tingling, until that seemed to wash away and she was suddenly sweating as if on fire. She waited several minutes, much longer than necessary really, listening for any sound that some other suitor-hunter followed the trail into the forest, and to be sure the group had gone.

Prince Carlton of East Cloudland! If Lily could have chosen a man for the bottom of the list of 59 suitors, Prince Carlton the Blabberer was it (just above the cruel and nasty Prince Alexander, naturally). He was not totally unattractive, but the moment he opened his mouth, her eyes had grown wide with boredom and disgust. He cared not a whit for anyone but himself, nor anything save hunting and its attire. His cruelty to Aaron on the hill just now made her blood boil, on a similar level to hearing of the fairies' circumstance. She hoped Aaron would be alright leading the troupe out of Jonquilline's part of the forest.

She gathered her courage and rushed back to the cave, anxious to tell the fairies and to get packed. Clearly they could not dawdle with their new friends any longer.

Lily shouted for the fairies when she neared the cave. They were up on the hill picking strawberries, and generally enjoying the perfect blue day. They flew down to meet her at the spring where she told them in halting breaths of Prince Carlton and their encounter.

"We must prepare to leave, at once," she finished hurriedly. "Aaron's gone to lead them off. I don't know for sure, I think," she faltered. "That is, I *hope* he won't say anything about me. He didn't when they asked directly, but that may have been the specific question more than anything."

"He doesn't know not to mention us, m'lady," Beloit pointed out.

"No, and I couldn't very well explain it to him while they were walking right below us."

"How're we to get through the forest if there's men already lookin' fer you here?" asked Marzipan, purple eyes going wide. "Hunters could be anywhere, m'lady."

"I hadn't thought of that," said Lily with a catch in her voice. Panic was really beginning to set in now. They could be anywhere, right this moment. She glanced frantically at all sides of the meadow, looking at every tree as if some bearded ruffian skulked behind each one with a knife in one hand and a veil in the other.

All of a sudden Lily noticed all the usual sounds of the forest – the birds, the chirping squirrels, the sounds of bugs – got quiet and faded away. At first she wasn't sure she saw it, but – wait – yes, there it was, something moving from one tree to the next on the far side of the lawn. Too fast to be a squirrel, too smooth of movement to be a bird. A flash of gray – or was it black? – floating from the branches of one tree to the next, jumping or flying, coming closer to the hill and the mouth of the cave. As it approached, she was sure it was gliding from tree to tree, jumping and spreading its tiny legs spread-eagle and gliding by little flaps that appeared along the sides of its body like a folding kite. One moment she'd see it glide – so quick! – between trees and then she'd lose sight of it in the foliage before it appeared again in some unexpected spot. A furry gray and black creature leaping through the leaves.

The fairies noticed it, too, and Beloit cried out, "It's a messenger! A sugar glider messenger!"

The messenger leapt from the nearest tree to alight on the edge of the spring with amazing precision and agility. Lily could see now it was indeed a small furry creature, gray with black stripes that ran from its nose down its back, a pink nose, large round black eyes, ears that pivoted toward the slightest sound, and a long furry tail. It's body was almost as long as Lily's hand but not as wide, its tail the same length again. It gripped the rocky lip of the pool with tiny hands that were clawed and hairy-knuckled. Something was tied around its neck by a leather thong.

Beloit and Marzipan started making very strange sounds, landing on the opposite side of the pool from the creature. They made little hissing, clicking, and tisk-tisking noises, almost as if imitating a bird or an insect. Then the creature answered in kind and Lily understood they were talking to it in its grumbling, questioning language. Then it stopped talking and let out a high clear bark, over and over, a small, round, sweet sound that for all its lightness carried very well.

Hearing the commotion, Jonquilline emerged from the cave where she had been napping. "Ah, my invitation has arrived!" she said with delight and said a tisk-click-click-tisk to the messenger in greeting.

The messenger apparently understood for it answered and then moved to a flat rock to one side of the pool. It hooked its hands under the leather thong and slipped its head out of the loop. The thong held a small pouch buttoned at the front, which the courier now opened using its teeth and opposable thumbs to pull the flaps apart. It slipped a folded sheet of parchment out of the pouch and proceeded to unfold it with its tiny pink hands, occasionally nudging the edge of the page with its nose when the paper didn't cooperate. Finally the parchment was laid flat on the rock and the messenger said something else and stepped away. Its duty apparently dispatched, it returned to the edge of the spring and bent a thirsty mouth to the water.

"Oh good, the Summit is planned for next week. I was

hoping my invitation would arrive soon," said Jonquilline, bending over the page.

Lily moved and looked at the paper the creature had delivered.

You are most cordially invited

To the 8th Annual Dragon Outreach Summit of the Enlightened Kingdoms

Castle Hadesburg, Hadesborough Kingdom

By permission of His Most Exalted Majesty, King Hal

By the grace and supreme planning of the Mistress of Ceremonies,

Queen Persephone Josephine Phoebe Phyllis the Fifth

Full Moon through New, Month of the Cherry Blossoms

Accommodations available care of the Hadesburg Dragon Lovers Guild.

Catering provided by the Fairies of Soula-May.

"Queen Persephone's Dragon Summit, yes, I read about it," said Lily, distracted.

"I attended last year," said the dragon. "I've been expecting an invitation by glider messenger to arrive any day now. I'm so pleased it came before you had to leave."

"Glider messenger?" said Lily. "Is that what that little fellow is?"

"That's the one. We use 'em in Soula-May to send messages over long distances," answered Marzipan. "We've domesticated quite a lot o' them. They're perfect for carryin' messages in the forest, glidin' as they do on their little flaps what go from wrist to ankle."

"We must be sure an' give him a go at our strawberry haul," put in Beloit, looking over at the glider who sat back on his haunches next to the spring. "They're sugar gliders, and they love anyfing sweet." He said something to the glider in its own language, and the glider answered and nodded its head vigorously.

"Oh, I do hope Maltese will be able to come this year," said Jonquilline, smiling at the invitation.

"The red dragon?" asked Lily before she could stop herself.

"You know of Maltese?" asked Jonquilline in some surprise. "Just how far have you three traveled?"

"From Starling," said Beloit. "We –"

"We came from Starling but are passing through to Hadesborough," interrupted Lily, glaring at Beloit for being a blabbermouth at a time like this.

"And how do you know of Maltese?" asked Jonquilline. "She lives in the north, as far as I last heard. Nowhere near Starling."

"Well, um." She looked away from Jonquilline's trusting black eyes, thinking she hadn't time for explanations, they should be going, going now. She turned back and decided to say it in the quickest way possible. "I have this book, that knows almost everything there is to know, and I was reading up on dragons," said Lily. It was the first time she had openly lied to the dragon.

Jonquilline looked Lily in the eye. "And this book that knows almost everything, it knows about Maltese the red dragon?"

"Um, yes," said Lily.

"I should very much like to see this book," said Jonquilline.

Lily started as she heard a noise in the trees behind her, and Aaron appeared on the path around the hill, completely soaked, covered in mud from neck to foot. He plodded up to the spot where the companions stood and, without ado, collapsed at the mouth of the cave.

A moment later, Aaron sputtered and spat at the water that Lily had thrown over his face. She slapped him soundly on the cheek, to which Jonquilline protested, saying he had a tendency to faint when he exerted himself.

"Give him some strawberries, Beloit, low blood sugar and all. There's a good boy," coaxed the dragon.

Aaron sat up and propped himself against a rock as he ate the proffered strawberries and sipped from the dipper. It was several minutes before he would answer Lily's pounding questions.

"It was those strangers," he said at last. "The ones you wanted to let go. I always knew there'd come a day when you'd need me, Jonny."

"And I'm sure you did a marvelous job, dear," assured Jonquilline. "Who were these strangers? What were they doing in this part of the forest? My, we seem to be getting a lot of visitors these days."

"They were looking for a princess who had run away. I guess her father told them to find her and that he'd give them gold if they brought her home."

"What did you tell them?" asked Marzipan, before Lily could ask the same question.

"I told them there weren't any princesses around here, of course," answered Aaron. "They wouldn't listen to me anyway. They thought I'd made you up, Jonny, didn't believe there was any dragon."

Lily, Marzipan and Beloit all sighed audibly.

"How did you get in this state of dishevelment, dear?" inquired Jonquilline.

"Well, I was leading them on the path that goes to the east toward Sweethaven, following the stream that runs out of our spring so I knew we were going away from the cave and not towards it. Then that nasty fellow in the stripes said he'd had enough of following my lead and pushed me into the stream. Got me wet and covered in mud. By the time I'd gotten up, they'd marched on. I trailed them a bit, but they were already headed toward the border and didn't seem to be turning back, so I let them go. Came back here."

Lily sat back with a huff against the rocks. He hadn't said anything about her, then. And even if he had, they weren't likely to believe him.

Jonquilline patted Aaron's hand with a green paw and looked at Lily. "I don't suppose you know anything about this missing princess, Violet?"

Lily gulped and did her best to draw on courtly manners once again to show a blank, innocent face. Well, maybe it was more from experience as a teenage daughter than courtly manners, for all that.

"No, nothing."

She continued to look Jonquilline in the eye until the dragon turned away. She didn't know if Jonquilline was satisfied, but at any rate the dragon let the subject drop.

"We've just received our invitation to this year's summit," she told Aaron, pointing to the sugar glider still perched on the spring's edge.

"Terrific!" said Aaron, perking up. "When will we be leaving, Jonny?"

"Oh, I suppose it depends on the plans of our guests." She smiled her green smile at the three travelers.

"Oh," said Lily, "don't change your plans on our account. We'll be going soon. We don't want the people fol- . . . . That is, we've got to get to Hadesburg and the halfway castle." She shared an uncomfortable look with the fairies.

"Yes, that's what I mean, dear. I think I should take you to the castle. Aaron can take the horse and Marzipan and Beloit can go with him and rendezvous with us."

Several cries erupted, Marzipan and Beloit with protest and Lily with delight. In the excitement the glider let out another bell-like bark.

"Wot'chu mean, shovin' me and my sister off onta this fellow while you abscond wiv our mistress?!" cried Beloit.

"No way 're we lettin' her ride on the back of a dragon we ain't known but three days," exclaimed Marzipan.

"Do you really mean I could ride on your back while you fly?" shrieked Lily.

"Rrrripf!" barked the glider (whose name, by the way, was

Penfold).

Aaron and Jonquilline turned to look at Penfold and laughed, silencing the torrent of questions.

"Do you mean that you would fly and I would ride on your back all the way to Hadesburg?" asked Lily. She couldn't conceal her excitement at the idea.

"Yes, that's precisely the way it's done. Most humans find it quite exhilarating, especially the first time," answered Jonquilline.

"It's jolly good," said Aaron. "It's the only way to fly."

"And just how're we s'posed ta get to Hadesburg?" asked Beloit angrily.

"Same way you've gotten this far," said Jonquilline evenly. "Riding in the saddlebags, or on Milwaukee's mane, or flying alongside. Aaron can care for the horse and get you through the forest. He knows the way."

"Are you sure?" asked Beloit, who sounded like he thought Aaron couldn't know anything so useful.

"Oh sure, I grew up not far from Hadesburg. Jonny and me go for a visit every summer after the summit," said Aaron, smiling at the dragon.

"Besides," said Jonquilline, "Aaron here's got a keen sense of direction. Back when he was still trying to slay me, I decided just to try losing him in the forest, since he obviously was more stubborn than the others." She chuckled a little in memory. "I led him to the deepest part of the forest, the dark part where you can't see the sun from the ground and can't navigate by it. There I chased him in circles, turning him around again and again. When night fell and I went back to my cave, I thought I'd seen the end of him."

"But next morning, she came out of the cave and found me drinking at the spring," finished Aaron. "That's when she offered me the job of bodyguard, asked me to stay."

"That's when I knew I couldn't get rid of you," said Jonquilline, laughing her waterfall laugh. "So clearly he won't get lost in the forest," she said, turning to Beloit and Marzipan.

Beloit looked unhappy but made no more protests.

"Beg pardon, m'lady, but I don't see as that's a good idea," said Marzipan to the princess. "We've only known these two fer a few days. A'course we like them and their hospitality has been grand, but that don't mean we should be splittin' up and trustin' dem wiv our lives."

"No, Marzi, you don't understand," said Lily. "I know I can trust Jonquilline." She turned and smiled shyly at the green dragon. "There's something I haven't told you, Jonny."

Untying the pouch from her waistband, Lily reached in and held up the Ring of Green Dragon's Dreams for all to see. "This ring lets me see your dreams, Jonquilline. I don't know exactly how it works, maybe the magic picks up the dreams of the green dragon nearest to whoever's wearing it, but I've worn it to sleep since we entered these woods, and back at the inn, that night the Book woke us up," she said to the fairies. "I've been dreaming your dreams. Or your memories. I'm not sure. That's how I know who Maltese is."

"Really," said Jonquilline quietly.

"Did Carlyle the bronze dragon, did he –" Lily paused, getting up the courage to actually say it. "Did he die that day you went out for Maltese's birthday?"

A sharp intake of breath, Jonquilline gasped and seemed stunned. When she let the breath out, twin tendrils of smoke floated from her nostrils. She was clearly upset. She closed her eyes and hung down her head in memory of grief.

"Yes," she said finally. "Carlyle died on Maltese's birthday. That happened. In fact, I dreamt of it a few nights ago, now that you mention it."

"That was the first night I wore the ring," said Lily.

"Now I see," said Jonquilline, nodding her massive head. "I've been feeling strange in my dreams lately, like I wasn't used to having wings, wasn't used to my body, and that explains it. I thought I was having flashbacks to the days when I would transform into a human, but it was you all along."

"Yes," said Lily. "So you see, there's no need to worry

about her taking me to the queen," she said to the fairies. "I've seen inside her dreams, I've *been* Jonquilline when I dream. I am absolutely sure I can trust her."

Marzipan looked at Beloit, asking a silent question. Beloit answered with a shrug. She rolled her eyes at her useless brother and turned back to Lily.

"So ye're seriously gonna ride this dragon's back all the way to Hadesborough? And you want us to go along on the ground wiv Aaron and Milwaukee? You don't want us wiv you?"

"It will be totally fine, Marzipan. I'm sorry you'll have to go the slow way, but it's really the best way." Lily leaned in close to whisper to them. "It means I can skip the part of the forest where people are looking for me. Besides, you know I can't trust Aaron to get Milwaukee there by himself. I need you and Beloit to go with him, see that they make it."

Marzipan's purple eyes were wide, and she was silent. After a long pause, she nodded.

"Good," said Jonquilline, "we're agreed. We leave tomorrow. Let's rest for the afternoon and share some sweets with the messenger."

Lily awoke early the next morning, as the first blue mists of morning were lighting the sky. She peered out the mouth of the cave, still laying in her bedroll, for some minutes. Everyone else slept soundly. Finally she got up and, clutching her cloak about her shoulders, went to the spring and drank from the dipper. Lily's ears prickled for sounds of men, or horses, pursuing her even in the dark, but the woods were quiet in the pre-dawn light. The trees that rimmed the clearing shimmered with silver dew. All color seemed stripped from the green valley in the pale blue light that made the whole sky glow.

What would it be like, to ride a dragon's back? She would have to remember to tie her hair back, not leave it down or the wind would tangle it. What would she do when she arrived at Queen Persephone's door? She gave another silent thanks to her new friend who would rescue her from the likes of Prince Carlton and his hairy comrades.

Would flying on Jonquilline's back be as wonderful as it was to fly in her dreams?

Before an hour after dawn had passed, they were ready to go. Milwaukee was brushed and saddled and Aaron was mounted on him. Lily had strapped her canvas bag to her back, and Jonquilline wore a leather harness of sorts that would give Lily something to hang on to. An unhappy Beloit and Marzipan hovered close to Lily, out of earshot of the others, refusing so far to sit down.

"I really am sorry it has to be this way, but it really will work out for the best," said Lily as sympathetically as she could. "It's the best way for me to get away from the suitors. For all we know these woods could be teeming with them."

"But it doesn't have to be this way!" protested Beloit. "We don't have to go wiv the knight! We could fly wiv you! There's no good reason fer us ta split up!"

Lily shook her head in anger. "Do you think we should just abandon Milwaukee, after he's brought us this far?"

"Wot about our safety?" asked Marzipan. "You said you were gonna protect us, that was why we came wiv you, and now you're leavin' us just 'cause you wanta fly." She waved her arm emphatically at the dragon.

"But you're in no danger out here! The men are looking for Princess Lily, not a couple of fairies! If you run into anyone on the way, you can just hide and everything will be alright."

Marzipan screamed in frustration, spinning around in the air and throwing her tiny hands up. Finally Lily put out her hand and scooped Marzipan up. She cupped her hands together till the fairy stopped battering around inside. Lily let her go and the girl stood on her outstretched palm, arms crossed.

"Do you want to tell me what's going on?" asked Lily simply.

"You're leavin' us, that's wot's happening."

"And just why are you and your brother so violently upset about it? I know Aaron's not the brightest companion, but he's perfectly nice and he'll be able to handle the horse, which you couldn't do." At this both fairies shot her angry looks. "I'm sorry to say it, but it is true. Are you going to tell me what the problem is? Because I haven't heard one good reason from either of you, just lousy complaints."

Marzipan looked Lily in the eye and put her fists on her hips. She huffed her breath out and finally said, "What if he catches us, m'lady? What are you going to say to Queen Persephone about us? What if she figures out who you've been travellin' wiv?"

Lily's steady gaze met Marzipan's purple eyes. "How is it you think he's going to find you, Marzipan? We don't even know he left the road and followed us into the forest. Even if he did, this is a very big forest. We have every reason to hope we've lost him. And if by some crazy twist of fate, he was to come across Aaron and Milwaukee on the way, you two would just hide, in one of the bags or flying out of sight. Wouldn't you? I mean there's no reason at all that the prince would know Milwaukee was the horse we stole."

Marzipan stared silently, looking glum, but finally said very quietly, "No, princess. I just don't like leavin' you."

"I know," replied Lily with tenderness, "I wish we could stay together, too, but hey, it's only for a week. We'll meet up again in Hadesburg."

Marzipan nodded, then seemed to resign herself and suffered a weak smile. She flew up off Lily's hand and flew back toward the horse, Beloit following silently behind her.

"Oh Marzi," called Lily. The fairy pivoted on her blue and white moth's wings. "Why don't you want me to tell Queen Persephone about you?"

Marzipan looked at the princess for a long time, as if making up her mind about something. "She's from Sweethaven, m'lady. Queen Persephone is Prince Alexander's sister."

Part Ten
In which The Starling Takes Flight

The fairies Marzipan and Beloit waved to Princess Lily as they flew away, trailing behind the knight on their horse. Lily turned to the green dragon Jonquilline and opened her mouth. She wanted nothing more than to talk about the amazing news that the person she was going to for counsel and guidance was the sister of the man she was fleeing. She wanted to sit down and consult the Book of Enlightenment, pore over it for an afternoon, and figure out why it was leading her in this tremendous circle. She couldn't bring herself to tell Jonquilline she had lied about why she was running away. She knew she had to fly on the dragon's back as soon as possible to get away from the many men pursuing her.

Lily shut her mouth and adjusted the straps on her pack. She climbed onto Jonquilline's wide back above her blue-green wings, settling her knees on either side and slinging herself into the leather harness. She wrapped the thick strap around her waist, and took instructions from Jonquilline on how to hook it around her arms.

"Ready," said Lily at last, letting out a breath of nervousness.

Jonquilline stood up very slowly, her ponderous bulk tossing Lily from side to side as she tottered and tried to balance. The dragon got to her feet and then bent her knees a little, bracing for take-off. The great wings unfurled to their full glory like the sails of a ship, the blue-green membrane ribbed with lines of emerald green the same shade as Jonquilline's ancient face. Lily marveled at the wingspan; it must be at least twenty feet. The great wings flapped, quick and light for their size, and Lily was gusted by a blast of air as they came down with tremendous force. Jonquilline beat her wings again and pushed off with her legs, ponderous and clumsy no more. They were up, they were floating slowly higher, every wingbeat buffeting the princess, who leaned forward and clutched the leather straps tighter in her delicate hands. Ten feet, fifteen feet, twenty feet off the ground and Jonquilline seemed to get serious all of a sudden, as the rhythm of beats went faster, faster than Lily could have imagined they would go with the amount of air they moved. They were above the treetops, and Lily could see the large boulders that were sprinkled through the meadow were arranged in a spiral. *Jonny must have dropped them, arranged them herself*, thought Lily.

They sped over the forest, the trees becoming indistinct blurs of green and black. She could see little rises in the landscape which had looked flat and unremarkable from the ground, could tell which trees were old and which were young by the amount each was gnarled and the color of their leaves. She could see a swath cut through the forest by some long-ago fire, all the trees young-green and small. They were passing the creek that ran off from the spring. Lily could see where it joined another creek, and another, silver ribbons wound around each other.

For the first few hours they flew over forest that was much the same. Lily learned the best way to balance without tiring out the muscles in her back and legs, and how to hang onto the leather harness in a way to feel safe but without chafing. Jonquilline found her pace and got used to Lily's weight on her back. She told the princess she was easier to bear to than the knight, because she didn't weigh as much and didn't fidget like he did.

As the terrain got rockier, Lily realized they were getting into the mountains. There wasn't much of a range left anymore, but there were many rolling hills and a few rocky peaks. Her eyes rested on one peak not far ahead, five miles maybe, that looked very familiar. With a shock she realized it was Mount Glorrin, and Jonquilline was heading straight for the top.

They circled the peak, wafting up on drafts of wind that blew up the mountainside, circling lower, till Lily could see a great rock ledge below them. Jonquilline landed, resting her back feet on the ledge and slowly steadying herself with her wings till her front legs touched down.

Lily unwound the leather from her arms and waist and slid off the scaly back. "It's Mount Glorrin, Jonny! I can't believe I'm really standing here!"

"Yes, it's quite spectacular. I remember when Mount Glorrin was just one of many peaks in this range, before the earthquakes took down the tallest of them. I was the one who named it, you know."

"What's Glorrin for? Where'd the name come from?" asked Lily as she paced around the ledge and looked at the vista.

"For my mother," whispered Jonquilline.

The view was amazing: it was a clear day without haze and the sky seemed to go on forever. Lily felt like she was on the highest point in all the world, that if she only knew what direction to look, she could see the Castle Starling, her home, or even the distant ocean. She remembered being on this spot on Maltese's birthday, and on the dawn of the last millennium, and in her childhood. It was very strange to remember these times that were not her own memories.

Jonquilline started a fire and caught some lunch. Lily enjoyed the food along with the wonderful view and uncommon companionship, but deep inside she was beginning to long for a normal meal and ordinary human society. The feeling passed as she listened to Jonquilline's stories of her childhood on this mountain, of her parents and friends, of a time when dragons were worshipped by country folk who left offerings to them fortnightly.

"Of course most of my friends are gone now. The dragon summit has some new faces, but I was among the oldest there last year. That's part of why I hope Maltese will attend, so I don't have to feel such an old lady with all those kids." She laughed shortly, a puff of smoke. "Most of them are less than 200! We have nothing to talk about."

"Well, I'll be there, Jonny. I know I'm not a dragon and I'm much less than two hundred years old, but I happen to think I'm pretty good company."

The dragon laughed, the sun glinting off the scales on her throbbing chest. "And so you are, my dear! But with you in the halfway castle and Persephone busy with the summit, I don't imagine we'll get to spend much time together."

"Oh," said Lily, "I suppose you're right. That means I won't be seeing much of the queen." She chewed her deer meat in thought.

"But that's not till next week. You'll have time to get settled in your surroundings and have some audience with the queen. She's very nice, you know. Her kind of charity cannot help but come from the heart."

"Wonder she doesn't come from a nicer family," muttered Lily.

"What's that, dear?" asked Jonquilline.

Lily looked up at her. "I was just wondering how she became so charitable. So many royals are not interested in helping lost girls or rehabilitating trolls. Why does Persephone do it?"

"Well, it's a delicate matter that is only whispered about in polite circles," answered Jonquilline, shifting a little uncomfortably. "Can I trust you are well-bred enough not to say anything when you get to the castle?" Her black eyes were wide and serious.

Lily took a deep breath and sat up very tall. "I assure you, I will use the utmost discretion."

Jonquilline's mouth curled at the ends, climbing up, the smile languorously reaching her eyes. "I thought so. Well, Queen Persephone herself had some trouble in her youth. She was not interested in courting young men and often ran off by herself when she knew suitors would be calling at the Castle Sweethaven."

Lily felt a sudden kinship with the young Persephone.

"She was sought after, very beautiful, very talented, but very selfish. Her reputation spread and a few suitors heard about her flights from court. So King Hal – that's the King of

Hadesborough, who was much older than Persephone – decided he was going to beat her at her own game, and instead of going to the castle himself, he sent a manservant dressed as a king and he waited outside the castle to see the princess flee. He rode after her and caught her in a field picking wildflowers. He took her back to his castle and kept her there as though she were his wife, sending word to her father and mother in Sweethaven.

"Persephone's mother, Queen Demi, was frantic about her daughter and came right away to Castle Hadesburg. She tried to insist that Persephone was not King Hal's wife, no matter what he said, but King Kazeus of Sweethaven knew it was over. He could see that Persephone could never marry anyone else, the word had gone round that she was already wed to King Hal, so no one else would have her, and that the best thing for her future was for her to become his queen officially. They were wed and Queen Demi threw many melodramatic fits, until finally King Hal agreed Persephone could visit for a few months every year.

"So you see, Queen Persephone realized she couldn't be selfish any more, that she must help other girls who had nowhere else to turn. Once the halfway castle was established, she started to branch into other charities, and here we are."

"But how could she live with the king who had kidnapped her?" asked Lily, aghast. "How could she endure it?"

"Well, King Hal is not entirely a bad man. He's just always been determined to get his way. Once Persephone was his, he softened toward her a great deal. He happily indulged her lost girl charity, laughing a little at it on the side. He wasn't so pleased at her other outreach programs, but he wanted to keep her happy, as she had grown rather powerful because of her popularity and good coverage in The Knightly Times. He wanted the press to portray him as kindly as well. Over the years they have grown fond, so I don't know that she herself would say things have turned out badly."

"But that's just so awful!" protested Lily, jumping to her feet. "Having to marry someone like that! Why didn't her father stick up for her? Think of *her* wants and not just reputation! What a family!" She shouted, her words echoing off the rocky mountainside.

"Persephone has mastered her situation very well and she is not bitter, so I don't see why you should get so upset about it. If she hadn't lived through such trouble and started her charities, you'd have no place to go," Jonquilline pointed out. She tilted her head and looked sympathetically at Lily. "Do you want to tell me what it is you're running away from?"

Lily huffed angrily. "I already told you. My father was going to make me marry someone who enjoys hurting people, and I couldn't stand that. Shouldn't we get going?" She began to kick at the coals of their fire to put it out.

"You didn't say he enjoyed hurting people. Why would your father choose such a man for his daughter?" Her rippling voice was calm and gentle.

Lily was stomping now on the ashes. "He – he didn't believe it about the pr- . . . about the man, so he didn't throw him out when he should have. Please, do let's get on."

"But surely your father cared about whether his son-in-law was cruel. How did you find out he was such a bad man if your father didn't even know?"

Lily kicked the last of the coals out. She looked up at the dragon, and gave her a tired, dusty look. "Please, Jonny."

Jonquilline sighed, but moved to the edge of the ledge into take-off position. "Let's go then."

They flew south. Lily's anger and indignance for Persephone's sake waned after a time. This meant that Persephone surely would understand her situation. Perhaps Alexander took after his father, and was selfish and mean-spirited. What would her own father have done? Sold her to King Hal if the price had been right, no doubt.

Oh, where was she going to go? After she made it to Hadesburg, if she managed to avoid being found out, would the queen send her home? Would Sir Scandalot be kind in his social column? What if someone like Prince Carlton or Prince Alexander, or even Burly or Grady found her there? Grady had said any man could be the one, but Prince Carlton had said it was only the men from her gala. Still there was obviously enough rumor flying about her flight and its ransom that any man on earth could be staking a claim. She touched her face, where that morning's application of wartberry had produced a few new lumps over her left eye, making it protrude and obscure her vision slightly. She only hoped it would be enough to keep people from looking too closely.

They came upon the river, a great blue road that wound through the forest, crowded by giant trees in places, open to the sky in others. At a wide spot with low vegetation, Jonquilline decided to give Lily's spirits a lift and flew very low to the water. The wings beat up, stretching over the banks and the trees in the mirror of the river. The wings beat down, stinging the surface, small as a bug tickling that wide silver skin. Jonquilline flew so low her feet hung a few meters above the river's surface, and the tips of her wings splashed into the water as she brought them down, like a drum beat, splash, splash, sending a spray over Lily's face and arms. Lily couldn't help laughing with exhilaration.

As they camped in a grove of aspen and ate their dinner, Lily pulled out the Book of Enlightenment for some much-needed answers.

First things first. "Tell me about the royal family of Sweethaven." The index fluttered, highlighting items for "Sweethaven, A History" and "Sweethaven, Royal Lineage," which had a subheading, "Prince Alexander of Sweethaven, see also Princess Lily of Starling."

Lily stuttered and asked to see that last one, amazed that information about her should be appearing in the Book.

> *Prince Alexander Channing Taron Bradley, eldest son of the royal house of Sweethaven, attended the coming-out party of Princess Lily Rose Violet Starling at Castle Starling along with 58 other royal and noble suitors. Prince Alexander, known for his affinity for fine books and his excellent horsemanship, attended Princess Lily's gala as*

*his fifth court appearance this year. To date he has not
asked for the hand of any of the ladies he has courted,
which The Knightly Times puts down to his desire for a
clever girl with a great imagination and a kind heart,
which, coupled with the perennial desires for beauty and
wealth, has been nigh impossible to find. The prince went
up against stiff competition for the Starling's only daughter.*

*Spectators' dreams of entertainment and intrigue were
thwarted by the unexpected departure of the princess on
the first night of the event. Due to an excess of Quattro
Centro wine at the gala, most attendees were uninformed
of this development until late the next morning, after
breakfast and several strong cups of coffee. Prince
Alexander apparently did know of the princess's flight, for
he left that same night. Sources have not yet been able to
determine where his intelligence came from, nor why he
should have chased after her. Spectators were much
enthused at King William of Starling's announcement that
all suitors should attempt to recover his daughter, and that
he would reward whomever succeeded.*

*Prince Alexander has risen above the reputation of his
father (who agreed to the wedding of his daughter,
Persephone, to King Hal of Hadesborough under much
duress) by involving himself in the charitable works and
summits Queen Persephone hosts. He has also hired
scribes and couriers out of his own funds to create libraries
and education centers for peasants throughout the
Enlightened Kingdoms.*

"But how can this be!" Lily said to herself, unable to
exclaim it loudly lest the dragon overhear her. She remembered
that Alexander said he'd brought her a gift made by scribes, so
that part could be true. And just because someone like books,
unfortunately that doesn't guarantee the person is good and nice
to fairies. Lily wished Marzipan and Beloit were there so she
could ask them. Then she had another idea. She flipped back to
the index. "Tell me about the Fairies of Soula-May." The item for
"Fairies" lit up, and several lines down under "Tribes" was the
listing for Soula-May.

The fairies of Soula-May occupy a realm in the forest region between the kingdoms of Sweethaven and Hadesborough. They are great chefs, bakers, dancers, firework-makers, storytellers and musicians. Most of their social life is based around week-long festivals . . . .

Lily skimmed past the information she thought she already knew.

Like all fairies, Soula-Mays have an average life span of 250 years. Unlike most fairies, Soula-Mays are mischievous and immature for the first half of their lifetimes, instead of getting over the rebellious stage in their 30s as many other tribes typically do. Soula-Mays tend to bend the truth to their own needs, and sometimes they are sent away to learn proper behavior in a castle or boarding school until they can conduct themselves well enough to join adult Soula-May society. Soula-Mays are clever and adventurous but selfish, and their practical jokes can sometimes get them in trouble, particularly with those not familiar with Soula-May society.

The text stopped there, with the next fairy tribe listed below it. Lily inwardly cursed the Book for not knowing more, but thought she might check it again tomorrow when she got to Castle Hadesburg, around more people who had experience with Soula-Mays. Marzipan had said she was about a hundred years old, so that must mean her mischievous days were behind them, didn't it?

Before noon the next day, they crossed into the plains of western Hadesborough. Lily looked back at the line of dark green where the trees rose so suddenly out of the earth. Facing forward again she looked at the plain they now flew over. So many textures of earth, grass, rock, crops. She could see farms with little stone cottages or thatch ones, friendly smoke spiraling out of chimneys, and even people, tending a garden or plowing by horse or herding livestock. The sheep were tiny puffs of white or black, each cow easily confused with a slow bush.

They started to see more cottages, and roads, and people

in wagons on the roads going by the cottages. Before long they were in sight of a village, round roofs happily cozying up to one another, a town square where merchants barked and shoppers bargained and beggars begged.

As Lily leaned slightly forward on Jonquilline's back to get a better look, she noticed what at first appeared to be a gang in one of the closer streets. Dozens of men, perhaps as many as 30 or 40, marched down the street, filling it from one side to the other. They were clearly from many different classes. Some were dressed richly, riding or leading horses, some looked middle-classed like merchants or money-lenders. Yet others must be bakers or fishmongers and even a few could be no more than beggars.

This strange troupe barreled down the street. The six or so in front were accosting women and girls in their path, ripping off cloaks and hats, dragging at braid and loose hair, grabbing wrists roughly and inspecting the girls' hands.

They were looking for someone. A young woman, in disguise.

Lily's hands began to shake. The leather strap slipped out of her right hand and dangled beside the dragon's scaly green neck. Without thinking, she leaned forward and grabbed at it, although the dragon's wingbeat kept it swinging out of her grasp. Just then Jonquilline banked to her right, heading for the castle Lily had glimpsed ahead. It was a gentle bank, but because Lily was already off balance as she stretched forward, and because her whole body was now shaking with fear of the mob she had seen, the princess slid forward abruptly on Jonquilline's neck. Her left foot caught the strap as she lost hold with her left hand. She screamed with ear-splitting clarity as she swung by one trapped foot off the flying dragon.

Jonquilline heard Lily's cry, since the princess's mouth was a mere handspan from her ear, and apparently so did many of the people in the village. Lily saw the mob pause in its marauding, and several men looked up at her. Two in the front seemed familiar, for all she saw them in a flash, one with a long beard and the other wearing a small, flat red hat.

Lily screamed again, in horror at the mob staring up at her, as much as at the very real prospect of falling in flight. She grasped again at the strap she had dropped, greatly impeded by the skirts that now flapped around her upside down form.

Jonquilline immediately sped up toward their destination, a large green lawn in front of the castle. She rolled slowly to the left, keeping her course but trying to get under the flailing Violet. I mean, flailing Lily.

Lily grabbed the strap at last and wrapped it around her hand several times, holding on for dear life. She strained and pulled herself toward the dragon's neck, trying not to move the foot that had secured her. At last Jonquilline had rolled enough that Lily got her legs wrapped around the poor dragon's neck, ankles hooked together.

"Violet? Violet! You can let go now, dear."

Lily opened her eyes a few moments later, tightly shut since her legs had caught hold. Jonquilline was standing in front of a very large castle, high walls concluding at an enormous gate some thirty yards away. Lily hung like a monkey to the right side of her neck, though Jonquilline had lowered her head enough that all she had to do was set her feet down in order to stand. She slowly disengaged her legs and stood up. Only after getting her feet firmly on the grass did she let go of the strap in her hands.

It wasn't enough, however. When she made to step away from the dragon, the strain rippled through her body and her knees buckles. She collapsed in a heap on the lawn, her overstuffed pack thumping her softly on the back of her head.

Lily took the moment of silence that followed to collect herself. They were here. Her hunters, her suitors, her stalkers, they were here, in Hadesburg, probably right this moment making their way to the castle. She thought she had escaped them, or at least gotten ahead of their pursuit, and she had been terribly, dangerously wrong. She mustn't let her guard down again.

Shuddering with the thought of those faces looking up as

she had screamed and hung off Jonquilline's back, no matter that she had been hundreds of feet in the air, she sat up quickly and brushed her hair out of her eyes. Jonquilline clucked over her with concern, but she managed to stand and settle her pack and gown back into place. Without a word and without looking at the crowd that had gathered, Lily strode toward the castle gates.

Two sentries stood in sight before the immense doors, polearms in hand, dressed in somber brown uniforms. The one on the left was young and had warm brown hair.

"Are ye all right there, miss? You almost took quite a fall there off your handsome ride," he said to Lily with concern.

"Fine" was all she could say through clenched teeth.

"I'm afraid I am quite skilled at containing the fall of a rider from my back in flight," said Jonquilline lightly. "Aaron's stumbling ways are not restricted to the ground."

Lily huffed and restrained the urge to give Jonquilline a murdering look, so embarrassed she was at being compared to the bodyguard. The sentry looked Lily up and down, as if assessing the damage for himself, then gave her a nod. He turned to Jonquilline.

"What is your business at Castle Hadesburg on this fine day, madam?"

"I am here to attend the Eighth Annual Dragon Outreach Summit," said Jonquilline. "I am Jonquilline of Glorrin. Violet, give the man my invitation."

Reading the slip, the young sentry said, "Good day and welcome, Jonquilline of Glorrin. Where's that fine blond fellow who accompanied you last year? Not fallen from too high a cliff, I hope. Is this your new servant?"

Lily blushed quite red at being called a servant, even to such a noble personage as the green dragon. She peered past the insolent young man.

"He's traveling by horse," said Jonquilline. "You should see him in a few days. This is Violet, a lost girl come to seek the queen's guidance and protection."

Lily wondered if this was some sort of formal way of

saying she'd come to the halfway castle.

"Ah, a new resident," answered the guard, looking at Lily again, and apparently concluding she did indeed look like a lost girl. "In that case, you may go in together, but she'll have to go on to the reception area. Can you point the way?" he asked Jonquilline. "If not, once you're inside, ask to see the concierge and he'll see her rightly home."

"Yes, I'm sure we can manage. Thank you," replied Jonquilline gracefully.

The other guard lifted a horn that was slung over his shoulder to his lips and tootled on it. A moment later the wide gate began to creak and move slowly inward as someone inside responded to the signal and cranked it open.

Lily walked through the gates beside Jonquilline, her eyes wide and ears keen with anticipation, her nervous hands clutched together in front of her. They walked under the great stone arch into a bustling community inside the Castle Hadesburg. Squires and messengers moved through the crowds at an eager pace. Servants and kitchen maids passed with their baskets of laundry and jugs of wine. Noble men dressed dandily stood talking and a few passed them on their way to town. A group of five or six fairies flew past chattering in a tongue Lily didn't recognize. There was an avenue between the outer wall and the first building, made of gray mottled stone that rose into the enormous round tower, making Lily dizzy as she gazed up at it. She had seen other castles beyond her own before, but still thought of Castle Starling as the norm. Her home was extravagant, but small and quiet, compared to this eruption of livelihood and conference and community.

She touched her bumpy face tentatively. Still disfigured. Good. She pulled some strands of her hair in front of her face anyway, and peered fleetingly out at the passersby for signs of trouble.

Jonquilline led them to the left around the tower, and eventually they met the long straight wall of the main body of the castle. An entrance opened into a cozy stone passageway, which led into an inviting lobby of yellow sandstone hung with tapestries. Jonquilline was able to fit through the entrance, but without much room to spare, so Lily was forced to walk behind her. As Jonquilline entered the lobby ahead of her, she heard the dragon exclaim with pleasure, saying some polite and formal greeting, and Lily heard an answering voice, murmuring an equally pleased hello. Jonquilline finally emerged into the room and left Lily enough room to get by.

"Violet, I was hoping I would get to introduce you myself. This is our gracious hostess, Queen Persephone. Your Majesty, please welcome my dear friend, Violet, who has come to seek your protection and guidance."

Before the dragon stood a tall elegant lady, dark rolling curls falling almost to her waist, wearing a slender golden crown woven with pearls, with a creamy complexion and large, serious, dark blue eyes. She was dressed finely but not too formally, this was an ordinary day at the castle, in a sky blue gown with a forest green overlay of silk and a woven belt with gold threads showing a delicate leaf pattern. The serious eyes looked Lily tiptoe to widow's peak, scrutinizing her, quickly analyzing the details of her dress and manner. Lily stood there nervously awaiting judgment, too frightened to speak or curtsy. She held the queen's eyes when they came back up to Lily's face, Lily's eyes turning brown in an instant.

Suddenly a broad smile appeared that made the dour power of her eyes recede as true warmth replaced it. She tilted her head and continued to smile approvingly at the princess, her long tresses falling over her bent elbow. Lily realized in a flash that they resembled one another, in coloring and loveliness, though clear signs of maturity showed in the lines about the queen's mouth and eyes when she smiled. And of course, Lily remembered, she hardly looked herself with the disfiguration of the wartberry.

"Welcome to my kingdom, my castle, and my home," said the queen sincerely. She reached out her hands and Lily took them a little hesitantly. "Is it your first time in Hadesborough?"

"Um, yes, it is," stammered Lily.

"Well, I hope you get to like it here. The other girls will be so pleased they have a new addition, someone they can show around town. And I'm sure you'll be popular in no time, with the story of flying on Jonquilline's back to regale them with."

Lily, who had never given a thought to trying to be popular in her life, mumbled something affirmative.

"And I can't wait to sit down with you and hear your story, so that we can get you started on rehabilitation and family placement, if that's what you need." The queen smiled kindly, and released Lily's hands. "I must remember to tell the healer to have a look at your rash." She smoothed one hand over Lily's lumpy cheek. "Ask the concierge when you meet him. We'll fix you right up.

"I'm afraid I'll be a bit busy with the dragon summit starting in a few days, but I'll make some time to see you before I get too swept away."

"Thank you," mumbled Lily.

"Now, Jonny, you're here early this year. Just to bring me a new sweet pea? And where is Aaron? Not broken anything important, I hope."

"No, Aaron's fine. He'll be here in a few days," said Jonquilline.

"Splendid. Have you time to help me with some decorating ideas in the southern courtyard?" asked the queen.

"Of course, your Majesty. In fact, I crave a word with you now that I've found you. That is, after we get Violet settled." Jonquilline nodded pointedly at the princess.

The queen turned back to Lily. "Yes, my dear, take that hall to the left, you'll see a door, then go up the stairs three flights, take a right, and go down the hall until you see the sign for the reception area. They can get you a room and take your information. We'll see each other soon."

Lily took a deep breath, and said, "Thank you so much for allowing me to stay, your Majesty. Your kindness is greatly appreciated and I look forward to an audience with you with great anticipation." She was terribly nervous from meeting the queen, exhausted from her ride and her almost-fall, and still trembling from her fright, but her courtly manners had not deserted her.

She turned and hitched her bag onto her shoulder, walking away as she heard Jonquilline begin, "There is a matter of some delicacy I wish to discuss with you. . . ."

Part Eleven
In which Princess Lily Becomes a Lost Girl

Alone, Lily walked down the hall, up the spiral staircase, up three flights. She paused at the window, taking the opportunity while she was alone on the stairs to retrieve some wartberry and rub a new supply on her face. She didn't want to risk being seen. There was no telling when she would be alone again. It itched instantly and stung a bit; she had apparently gotten some scratches when she landed.

Were the men already arriving at the castle? Would they be inquiring after Princess Lily? Perhaps they didn't know this was her destination. In fact, they couldn't, not without guessing, or torturing Martha, the only person besides the fairies who knew. Would Prince Carlton and Lord Burly be smart enough to ask after any new Lost Girls in the halfway castle? Lily crumbled the remains of the wartberry out the window and dusted her hands on her dirty dress.

The last flight up, another heavy wooden door, and a hallway that seemed to go on with no end. Lily was suddenly very tired, feeling all the muscles she'd used in clinging the dragon's back, feeling the lack of a tasty meal, and the utter lack of featherbeds since she'd left home nearly two weeks ago. At least the trembling had begun to wane.

She looked up and saw a painted wooden sign that hung on a rod into the hallway, and stopped when she got under it. She looked to her right and saw an empty wall, and looked to her left and saw an alcove with a blonde girl sitting behind a counter. The girl seemed to have been waiting for Lily to notice her and flashed a smile when she turned around.

"New admission?" she asked.

Setting down her pack with a heavy thud at her feet, Lily nodded.

"Anything you'd like to declare?"

Lily shook her head uncomprehendingly. "I'm very tired," she declared.

"That is, anything in your baggage to declare? Any alcohol, pipeweed, live animals, that sort of thing?"

"No." Lily shook her head. "No, nothing like that. I have fairy servants, but they're not here yet."

"Well, we'll just have to log them in when they arrive." The girl picked up a quill and held it at the ready over a clean scroll of parchment. "Name?"

Lily hesitated, then decided to lean close and whisper, "Listen, I don't know how it works here, but I really can't give you my real name, at least not all of it. People are looking for me."

The girl shook her head. "Your records are confidential. No one but the queen and a few administrators ever see them."

Lily bit her lip, but said, "My name is Violet. That's all I can tell you."

The blonde eyebrows rose skeptically, and the girl gave Lily a disapproving look, but wrote the name down anyway. "Reason for seeking guidance and protection?"

"Arranged marriage," Lily said simply. Given the queen's background, this should be sufficient reason for running away. She answered several questions in the same vein.

The girl finished the scroll, rolled it up neatly and placed it in a pigeon hole in the wall behind the desk where hundreds of other scrolls were pigeon-holed. She went to the door beside the reception alcove and said, "Come with me, please."

The girl showed Lily around the wing (specially built for the halfway castle, she said), including a Common Room for relaxing in the evenings in the cushy velvet chairs, and she pointed to the staircase that led to their private dining room.

"This is the dressing room, which is where we dress every morning and also where you'll get your new gowns fitted. Is that the only dress you have?" she asked, nodding her head at the one Lily was wearing.

Lily looked down self-consciously at her gray linen

archery dress, quite rumpled from her fall, and a bit dirty where she had lain on the lawn. Smoothing the fine, sturdy fabric over her hips, she said, "I have another with me. I should be getting another two with my friends who will be arriving soon."

The blonde girl didn't seem to believe her, but said, "Well, most of us come with only the clothes on our backs. *You* must have had time to pack." This last she said a little maliciously. "When we arrive, the queen sends the tailor to make us a few dresses, for work and for special occasions. I suppose she'll decide whether you need any."

The next room down the hall had a closed door, and the blonde girl made no move to open it. "These are our private chambers. If you need some special kind of furniture, a spinning wheel or a writing desk or a treadmill, you can make a request of the concierge. Ah, here's your room."

She turned the knob on a door marked 17. Lily noticed there was no lock. The room was much smaller than the room Lily had had at home, but it *did* have a featherbed, thank goodness! And a small dressing table with ewer, basin, and a hand mirror. Above the dressing table was a window at chest height, looking out onto a large courtyard ringed by more of the castle wall.

"It's very nice," said Lily, looking longingly at the bed. "Thank you."

"Of course. Welcome to Castle Hadesburg," said the girl, tipping her head formally.

"Are you a . . . a resident here?" asked Lily hesitantly.

The girl met her with a straight brown-eyed look. "Yes. We all work here, you know. The queen has us tutored and counseled and we have a lot of free time, but we all must work in some fashion to stay here. The queen is a firm believer in a woman standing on her own. Today is my day in reception. Are you hungry?"

"Yes."

"Set your things down, and I'll show you to our dining room. The other girls will be mostly finished, I expect, but some might stay to talk to you if we hurry."

"Thank you," said Lily again, setting down her bag and following the girl out the door. "What's your name?"

"Caroline," answered the girl, looking straight ahead.

The dining room, down a flight of stairs and adjacent to the kitchens, held two long wooden tables with benches that took up most of the room. About half a dozen girls sat at one table chatting, all but one finished eating. When Lily and Caroline came in, they stopped talking abruptly and looked up.

"Who's this?" said a girl with strawberry blonde hair down her back and a pointy nose. "Have you brought us a new cat, Carrie?"

Caroline looked annoyed, but answered, "This is Violet. I've brought her down for some supper. Is there any left or do I have to call the cook back?"

"There should be some left. Why don't you bring her a plate?" prompted the red-haired girl, patting the bench beside her as her eyes fixed on Lily.

Caroline made a low rumble of discontent but went through the door at the far end of the room. Lily smiled and sat down next to the red-haired girl, saying hello to the others at the table.

"I'm Aalyn," said the red-head. "This is Shorty, Narnia, Catherine, Joanna, Sabine and Buttercup. Are you the one that nearly fell off of the green dragon?"

Lily was embarrassed that word had traveled so quickly about her disgraceful entrance. "Yes, I arrived just a little while ago. When she got her invitation to the summit by glider, she offered to bring me here. Oh, thank you so much," she said to Caroline who set a plate of steamed vegetables and half a roasted chicken in front of her. "You really didn't have to do that."

"Aren't you going to join us and chat with the new girl?" asked Aalyn in a sing-song way, slightly too sweet to be sincere.

"No, I'm going to the library, now that reception is closed," said Caroline over her shoulder as she walked swiftly out.

"Don't worry about her," said Aalyn to Lily. "She's in a bad mood this week. Her beau was out with another girl and she can't get over it." Aalyn and the other girls were overcome with giggles.

"Naw, tis two weeks since his adventure started," said Narnia, a younger girl with straight brown hair and a pleasant face. "She rushes out to get The Knightly Times first every week so she can read about him before we can."

"You see, Caroline has had a big crush on Prince Alexander since she first came here two months ago," explained Aalyn. "The queen has found her several prospective husbands, but it never works because she's holding out for Alex."

"Really, mmm," said Lily. Delighted she had her dinner to cover her reaction, she stuffed another spoonful of peas into her mouth.

"I don't know who she thinks she's fooling. He's nice to her, but he's nice to all us poor unfortunates. She's not even noble, there's no way a prince is gonna marry her. She's been in this rotten mood ever since she heard the prince was going to The Starling's court to meet the flighty Princess Lily. And when she heard he was chasing after her! Oh, she's just been unbearable."

"I just wish she'd stop trying to smarten up for him. 'I'm going to the library'," said Sabine in a mockery of Caroline's voice and laughed.

Lily's eyebrows rose and her eyes turned hazel as she stared at the girls over her drumstick.

"Have you heard the latest about Princess Lily?" said Aalyn.

Lily mutely nodded her head, not too vigorously.

"Of course, she's a complete fool for running away, not just from a fellow as fabulous as him, but I heard there were 50 other gents there! Imagine the choices she must have had," said Aalyn, shaking her head in disapproval.

"I heard it was 58," muttered Lily to herself.

"Apparently, a whole lot more than that have taken up the King's challenge. I heard he offered her hand and fifteen thousand gold pieces to whoever finds her. Can you imagine any girl being worth so much?"

"I rather feel sorry for the poor girl, should she ever be caught," put in Buttercup. "Her father's practically sold her on the open market."

"Oh, it's not as bad as that," assured Aalyn. "It's only the gents from her gala that can claim the reward, so it's not like she'll be forced to marry any bloke off the street."

"Forced to marry, nonetheless," said Buttercup.

"Is it, um, only the blokes from her party, though?" asked Lily haltingly. "I've heard a couple different versions, that any man who found her could do it."

"Well, that's what The Knightly Times said," replied Aalyn. "Though I know you can't believe everything you read in the papers. You'd think all that competition would make Caroline calm down. We just know she's hoping the prince will show up here, without Princess Lily, of course."

"You've all met Prince Alexander?" asked Lily, looking around the table.

"Oh yes. He's very charming, and well-read," said Aalyn.

"Takes after his sister," said Narnia.

"Beautiful eyes," said Buttercup.

"And he's marvelously kind," said Joanna.

"Does he, but, um," stuttered the princess. Regaining her composure, she said, "Have you ever seen him with his servants? Is he kind to them?"

The girls burst out with several affirmative answers at once: he was well-loved by his servants, whenever he came he saw they were fed before he was, he just couldn't be kinder.

Lily shook her head in bewilderment, sorry there was no more dinner to hide her face. These people were sorely mistaken. Like Beloit had said, just because a man was charming, doesn't mean he's not a pig. She wished the fairies were with her, to set these poor lost girls straight.

Before she could think of anything else to say, the door at the other end of the dining room opened and the queen walked in. The girls all stopped talking and stood abruptly, standing up straight with their hands clasped demurely behind their backs. Belatedly, Lily rose and assumed the same posture as the queen approached.

"Good evening, ladies. Supper was enjoyable, I hope," said the queen, looking up and down the ranks and smiling.

"Yes, thank you, your Majesty," said the girls in unison.

The queen took Lily by the crook of her arm and said, "You'll learn the routine soon enough, my dear." She steered her toward the door. "Good evening, ladies."

"Good evening, your Majesty," said the girls together.

Lily and Queen Persephone walked together through the halls of the castle until they were in the courtyard at the back, the one Lily had seen out of her bedroom window.

"Now, my child, how is it you heard about our program?"

Would mentioning the Book of Enlightenment give her away? Better not to risk it. As far as Lily knew, it was the only one of its kind and was likely tied up in her own growing legend.

"Your reputation for helping lost girls is great, your Majesty, even beyond your kingdom. I heard about the halfway castle from a cottar I stayed with after leaving home," said Violet. I mean, Lily.

"I see," said Persephone. "And what is it you have run away from?"

"My father had arranged for me to marry someone I believed at the time I could not live with."

"At the time?" said Persephone. "Have you changed your mind since running away?"

"N-no, your Majesty. I'm just not sure what will happen to me. And I miss my family."

Persephone looked at Lily, studying her face. "Of course you do, dear. Have you any interest in marriage? Or was it merely the man your father had picked whom you couldn't tolerate?"

"I don't really know, your Majesty. I think I would like to be married, if I could find the right man," said Lily honestly.

"And how would you know the right man if you met him? What qualities are you looking for?" asked Persephone. They continued to stroll around the outer wall of the castle along the edge of the courtyard.

"I would like someone who enjoys books as I do, and learning about different cultures and societies. I want someone who looks at the positive side of things, who tries always to do the right thing even when it's not the easy thing. And he absolutely must be kind," said Lily.

Persephone smiled. "The man you described sounds a lot like my brother. That is if you also like someone who's handsome and loves horses?"

Lily swallowed hard and managed to say yes.

"Have you ever heard of Prince Alexander of Sweethaven? I'm from Sweethaven originally, you see. Jonny probably told you that. I visit my mother there every year, and my other brothers, but Alexander is the only one with whom I'm close. He helps out at my functions when he can." Persephone sounded quite fond of her younger brother.

"Do you expect him at the summit, your Majesty?" Lily asked bravely.

"I don't actually know. He talked of coming last I heard, but he's out . . . adventuring at the moment." Persephone's face quirked into an uneasy smile. Lily hoped sincerely that she was not about to hear another horrible thing about herself.

"The girls in the dining hall were talking about him before you came in, actually," said Lily. "They seem to like him."

"Oh yes, at least one too much." She turned to the princess. "You think I don't know about Caroline's crush? I know all that goes on in the lives of my girls. I've told Lex not to encourage the girl, she's been impossible to place because of him, but he just can't bring himself to be cruel and push her away, even though it's for her own good."

"Well, she does seem quite unhappy about it," offered Lily, thinking unkindly that a sourpuss like Caroline deserved such a wretch for a husband.

"She's just not lively enough for him, hasn't enough sense of self. Lex needs a woman who knows what she wants and won't try to change herself to be what people expect of her." She gave Lily another sidelong glance. "Listen to me, prattling on about other girls' crushes and the character of my brother. You don't want to hear about that, I'm sure."

When the queen paused, Lily said, "No, it's all very interesting, I assure you."

"You are very kind. What do you think of our arrangements?" asked the queen, gesturing to include the bowers and tables set up in groups around the enormous courtyard, with a little stage in the center before a great open circle, and garlands of greenery slung on the wall all the way around. "We're putting up banners and booths tomorrow, but I think it's a good start."

"Oh, yes, it's lovely. I suppose you can't have a summit for dragons indoors, can you?" observed Lily.

"No, Violet, you can't. Jonny can only fit in certain parts of the castle. She's not the largest guest by far."

Closing the door to her bedroom some time later, Lily realized suddenly that it was the first time she had been alone in weeks, truly alone without a friend or servant within earshot. She missed Martha acutely, wishing her handmaiden were there to talk to her, as someone who could see the truth about people without being taken in by treachery.

Lily skimmed over the material in the Book of Enlightenment about Prince Alexander, all of it proclaiming his wonderful qualities, his love of books and kind treatment of horses, his charm and his debonair style. Lily imagined for a few moments what such a prince would be like, in real life and not just the gloss of celebrity. He might look like Prince Alexander, with those soft dark curls and kind eyes, who after all was certainly handsome to look at. If only he had a kind heart to go with them, she thought, if only the stories her fairy friends had told her weren't true somehow. She wished by some miracle it was all a misunderstanding and the outward shell of a good man wasn't concealing hidden evils. Then maybe she could share her passion with such a prince, instead of warring with him over it. Lily's girlish fantasies carried her all the way to thoughts of Caroline and her crush on Alexander's good-man-shell, and even allowed herself a little jealousy at that innocent affection.

Tired of thinking about the fellow who had pushed her into this whole adventure, she asked the Book about the price on her head. The Book seemed confused for a few moments, flipping at first to "price," and then "ransom," and – for reasons Lily couldn't fathom – "mince meat." It finally settled on an entry for "Starling, Royal Lineage," under which her name appeared. It seemed to have not only the information Lily had been told, but many different versions of the same rumor. The King had offered five thousand gold pieces, ten thousand, or fifteen thousand to the man who found his daughter. He had offered the reward only to a choice set of men from the gala, or to all of the original suitors, or to any noble person who had missed the party, or to anyone at all. He had offered her hand in marriage, to be betrothed upon her safe return, or a week of chaperoned courting, or a bit of land in the kingdom that he rarely used and would allow the man to court his daughter alongside all comers. He had proclaimed it from the gallery, or over dinner in the Only Slightly Grand Hall for Barely Special Occasions, or shouted it down at the Rose Vine Courtyard as the men were getting on their horses and riding away.

It even had a quote from her father from the paper:

> *"I am setting this bounty only for the safe return of my one and only beloved daughter. Anyone pursuing her should ensure that she comes to no harm. Also, be on the lookout for a pair of fairies who are maliciously cahooting to keep her in the dark with their ridiculous stories."*

Lily could imagine her father's voice perfectly with these words. While she worried what would become of Marzipan and Beloit if King Henry ever got his hands on them, she couldn't help seeing his affection in his words. If only she could sort the truth from the rampant fictions. It would be so nice to believe he had limited the call to arms, and not said she'd marry her captor straight away. A few tears trickled down our princess's lovely cheek, frustration and anger and desperation and dim hope all swirling around in her brain. She tossed the Book across the room, where it struck the door and fell open on the floor.

The next morning, the castle was astir with talk of the arrival of several princes the previous evening. Sometime after dark, after Lily and Persephone had spoken, Prince Carlton Shelton Lewiston Worthington of East Cloudland, and Lord Burly Jesterfoot of Southern Lualdath, at the head of a company of 32 men, had arrived at the gates and demanded housing for the night. The queen had agreed gracefully enough, but the servants tittered in all the corridors that the lady of the house was incensed. Offering shelter and food was one thing, certainly it must be done for nobility, but they were asking all sorts of unseemly questions about her Lost Girls!

At breakfast, Lily listened attentively to all the gossip. At the end of the meal, an officious little man with a monocle and a barrel chest entered the dining room, setting a bar in the door after closing it behind him. Aalyn whispered to Lily that this was the castle concierge, Mister Zidler. The girls hushed their chatter and looked up at his polite "Ahem."

"Good morning, girls," he said in a high, slightly squeaky voice. "I know you all are used to starting your etiquette class at this time, but there has been a change of plans. Or rather, venue. Rather than meeting in the Terrific Hall this morning, Mistress Selway will conduct your class here. You must all be good girls and help the staff clear the tables first. Then, when it comes time for your duties this afternoon, they will be held in the halfway castle wing, mostly sewing and mending tapestries, rather than your usual rounds. Reception is also closed for the day."

"Mister Zidler," said Narnia, raising her hand, "will we be allowed to go out in the rest of the castle? I wanted to return my book to the library and get another one."

"No," said the concierge. "I'm afraid all your activities for the day will be restricted to the halfway castle wing, and this dining hall, of course."

"Is this because of the men searching for Princess Lily?" asked Aalyn boldly. "Do they want to see us so they can pull our hair and see if she's here in disguise?"

Several girls laughed at this.

"I'll bet the queen doesn't want to let them near us," twittered Shorty.

"If they're all bachelors, I say let them in!" shouted Buttercup, to great shrieks and applause.

"I don't see why they can't just see us and then they'll know Lily isn't here," sneered Caroline. "None of us look anything like her. Then they could stop interrupting our lives."

Meanwhile Lily was hunching forward and hiding beneath her hair, trying to fold in on herself and escape notice.

Zidler tittered and settled them down again. "Now, it's nothing like that, girls, please calm down. There are many strangers coming in for the Dragon Summit, and with all the preparations, Her Majesty thought it best that you remain out of the way. That's all. No more of this Princess Lily hoopla, please." He gave the room a curdling look over his eye-piece.

The girls began clearing away the breakfast things more or less in silence. Lily was surprised to see Zidler approach her.

"You must be Violet," he announced. "The queen told me about your rash." He peered at her face, squinting in inspection. "It does seem quite pronounced. Is your face usually so lumpy? It's allergic reaction, unless I miss my guess."

"No, sir, um," mumbled Lily, trying to sound as timid and un-royal as possible, "this is mostly how I looks anyways. Just a bit itchy right now, 's all."

"Well, the queen said I should send the healer to you. Tomorrow?" When she nodded meekly, he bowed abruptly and turned on his heel, leaving the room.

That evening, Lily was lucky enough to have an audience with the queen, who closed off the Common Room in the halfway castle for their talk. Persephone talked about her brother, regaling Lily with tales of their youth and his help with her many charities. Lily asked a few pointed questions about whether he was anything like his father, being careful not to let slip her ideas about what kind of man King Kazeus was for marrying off his daughter as he had. Persephone even opened up about her marriage to King Hal, who did not seem in evidence in the castle.

"No, he's out hunting until the summit begins in a few days. He'll come back just in time. I like to keep my girls to myself anyway," said Persephone.

"Does he not like you having us here?" asked Lily.

"He honestly doesn't care. Hal's all right as long as you know how to keep him happy." Persephone ruefully shook her head.

Lily couldn't stand it. She had to know. "How can you do it? How can you stay with him? Jonny told me what he did, kidnapping you –"

"Ah!" Persephone held up her index finger to Lily. "Stop right there. The legend has my story greatly out of proportion, as I'm sure you can understand, so don't go believing everything you hear about me and Hal. He did not kidnap me."

"What??"

"He found me in the field of wildflowers where I would go when I ran away, but he just came and talked to me, charmed me actually." She smiled a little in spite of herself. "He made up fabulous stories to entertain me. He told me I was lovely enough to be a princess, to be queen of his world. You see, we were both pretending not to be royal at first, since I had run away and he had given his kingly robes to his manservant. So we flirted in the grass and played tag and climbed trees, and when the sun went down and I said I should be getting back, he offered to let me ride his horse with him.

"Well, it is terribly improper for an unmarried lady to ride on the same horse as a man, but I already liked him so much I thought it would be alright. He headed away from my home and I was even more excited about what could happen. I didn't tell him to turn around."

"So he did kidnap you! He got you on his horse and rode

away with you!" protested Lily.

"That he did, but a princess can't always speak up for what she truly wants. It was wrong that he didn't ask my permission before he swept me away, but if he had, I might have forced myself to say no, just to be proper. Perhaps I should have known what he was planning, but now I see, first impressions are almost never wrong, they're just incomplete. Hal *is* a very charming individual, and very entertaining, and he certainly does find me lovely. He's far from being the worst man I could have married. He's just selfish and immature, sullen and tempestuous. So I let him go on his hunting trips before my events and show up right before they start, welcoming him with loving arms," she spread her arms wide for an imagined embrace, "and he lets me hold my events and charities and tells me what a brilliant job I did afterward. It's really all for the best." Persephone looked at Lily directly and seemed earnest.

"That's what Jonquilline said, that you didn't mind it any more," said Lily.

"And so I don't," said the queen. "I wish that every woman could choose the person she spends her life with, that's one of my aims with the halfway castle, but the other is to teach young women to understand what they truly want, and make it happen in her life. Don't go through the years of fighting and regret and anger before coming to terms with your life the way I did. We all make choices, and sometimes the choice that affects us the most is not who to marry or where to live, but how we live the life that's given to us. Fight for the changes you want that are in your power, but make peace with the ones that are not. And of course, do your best to figure out which is which."

Lily sighed, taking it all in. "You're a very wise lady, your Majesty. These girls are lucky to have you."

A queer smile came over the queen. "And you? Are you not lucky to have me, also?"

Lily smiled too, wondering grimly how this wonderful woman could help her escape her twisted circumstance. "Me most of all."

Part Twelve
In which We All Meet Again

I t was three days before the house arrest was lifted on the Lost Girls. Lily continued to see Persephone in the evenings, sometimes for an hour or more, and the queen continued to talk about her life and her brother. Lily grew to dread any mention of Alexander. It was hard to keep nodding and mm-hmming at all the wonderful things Persephone had to say about him. Sometimes she thought Alexander must be a mighty actor to keep his cruel side so well hidden from such a wise, well-rounded lady. Other times she allowed herself back into the girlish fantasy where he had only good qualities like the ones his sister described, and this magical non-existent prince was in love with her.

While I'm at it, she thought, I might as well imagine minstrels I can carry in my pocket or a way to send a message instantly to another kingdom. These thoughts always brought her back down to earth.

Finally the girls were allowed into the rest of the castle. The word passed to them that the ominous visitors remained in residence, staying at the castle at night and foraying into the surrounding country for their search during the day. The girls were given strict instructions to avoid all contact with these men, and any other strangers at the castle for the summit. They were not allowed to talk about their life as Lost Girls, and on no account were they to mention how long any of them had been staying at Castle Hadesburg.

Lily continued to apply her wartberry, daily now to ensure her disfigurement would not fade. The healer came around to see her at last, and offered, as she expected, a drink of rose leaf tea. She pretended to gratefully accept it, and poured it into her chamber pot the moment the healer left her alone.

The castle was so crowded with conventioneers, the princess-in-hiding could hardly make her way through the halls, thronged as it was with farmers and nobles and dragon lovers. After waiting for the crowd to move for fifteen minutes, she finally made it to the bottom of the stairs on the ground floor. Seeing the entrance hall and the sheer amount of sweaty man-flesh packed in, she decided she would try her luck in the avenue outside. At least that had fresh air.

Lily made her way around the building and the great tower, saying hello to people she had met in the last few days. She passed the castle gates which were equally thronged with people, and glanced at the crowd for any sign of Aaron or the horse. As she was about to give up, a horse came up alongside her, going the same direction as she was. She saw the dark lustrous brown hair, saw the familiar saddlebags with the Starling crest, and looked to the horse's head for the white spot under the forelock for confirmation.

"Milwaukee!" she thought with excitement, unable to cry out her familiarity. She threw both arms around his neck. He stopped moving forward and stood still for the cuddle. "But where's Aaron?" she asked the horse, letting go and stepping around front to see who was leading him.

He stood there in a dusty blue tunic and light brown breeches, brown curls held back out of his eyes with a leather thong. Prince Alexander's leather-gloved hand gripped the reins right next to her face. His broad shoulders squared themselves as he looked at her. She could see the muscles of his thighs tighten beneath the riding breeches as he stood up straight.

A cold thrill flashed through her whole body, followed directly by a hot tingle everywhere as their eyes met for a moment in which all the bustle seemed to fade away until he and she were the only ones standing in the avenue, in the castle, in universe.

"Hello," Lily said.

"Hello," said Prince Alexander.

After a moment, he said, "Are you lost?"

"Pardon?" she asked, backing away from him.

"Are you a Lost Girl? Here at the castle?" he asked again.

She stuttered, remembering the command that she not say how long she had been there. Not that she wanted to reveal anything to this man. Where were the fairies? How did he get hold of her horse?

"I ask because I was wondering if you know the way to the stables. I need to settle my horse, before I go see my sister," he said, boring into her with a dark brown gaze.

"I . . . I know the way to the stables, yes."

"Good. I am Prince Alexander of Sweethaven. Tell the stable master, will you." He handed her the reins, still looking straight into her eyes. She took the reins without a word, and did not look away.

He hadn't recognized her. With a courteous nod, he passed on toward the main tower, and did not look back.

She stood there in the avenue, holding the reins of her horse. She was dressed in her new frock provided by the halfway castle. The only pair of boots she had were on her feet, perfect for riding away in, which she had already done once with this very horse. The only possession she would be sorry to leave behind was the Book of Enlightenment, stowed under her bed in her room.

A kitchen maid passed her, gossiping with a companion. "It'll only be a matter o' days before he figures it out. Prince Carlton is a right clever bloke, despite his obsessive nature. In fact, I bet tis that same way of obsessing gets him in to view the Lost Girls. He's already tried bribing me friend Brigid, to get into the dining room. Mark me words, any day now, he'll get in to see them."

Lily was off through the castle gates before the maid was out of sight. The sentry said hello, the same young fellow who had greeted her and Jonquilline.

"Hello, miss. Have you seen young Aaron? He's arrived, only just a little while ago."

Lily cringed inside at the fact that she now had a witness

of her flight – that is, her second flight, or third, if you count Jonquilline, you know – but she put on a bright smile for the guard.

"Yes, I was just doing him a favor. Seems his horse has thrown a shoe. I'm taking him into town to get him reshod."

The guard stared at the horse's legs and Lily hoped instantly that she hadn't gone too far, and that he wouldn't think to look for Milwaukee's shoes.

"There's smiths in the castle can do that, miss. In the royal stables."

"Of course," said Lily, tilting her head coquettishly to the side, "but Aaron is from Hadesburg. He insisted I take the horse straight to his cousin, who is an apprentice blacksmith. Said he'd never be forgiven if he took his business elsewhere."

The sentry furrowed his eyebrows, but then he began slowly to nod his head. Clearly family matters were more important than convenience.

"Off you go then. Good day."

"Good day to you, sir," replied Lily sweetly, leading Milwaukee with a slight skip down the street into the town.

As soon as she could duck into an alley out of sight of the castle guard, she mounted Milwaukee, who still wore her Starling saddle. On the road into the hills north of the castle, she galloped.

The countryside surrounding the city of Hadesburg was mostly low, rolling hills which had occasional spiky stones protruding in long wandering lines. Sparse coniferous woods played in the shadows of these spines, getting thicker as the elevation climbed. Most of the hills were covered in swaying yellow grass, but with spring in full swell, the wildflowers were hitting their prime. Some hillsides wore mottled skirts of purple lupines, yellow prairie lilies, and red poppies. Lily gasped in wonder as she came upon an entire hillside dressed in bright blue flax, the long stems dancing in the wind like waves of a foreign sea.

Lily dismounted and walked the horse, finally relaxing

from her tense morning. Then she heard voices coming from the saddlebags.

"Are we there yet?"

"Oh, good goblins, where are we?"

Marzipan pushed the leather flap open and braced one arm over the side of the saddle bag. Beloit's mossy head appeared next to her as he stood up and looked around.

"M'lady!" he shouted. Then both of the fairies flew like mad fireflies at the princess, hugging her neck, kissing her cheek, fluttering about her hair. Lily was so excited to see them that she wished for the moment it was a reunion with someone big enough to hug.

"How did you find us, m'lady?" asked Beloit. "We was wiv the prince."

"And where the bloody heck are we, now ya mention it," said Marzipan, hovering with her hands on her hips, looking at the hillside trail.

"I'm so glad to see you! I have to admit I forgot about you for a little while, I was so busy concentrating on getting away from Castle Hadesburg without being seen."

"Away for Castle Hadesburg?" said Beloit with some alarm. "Why're you running away from Castle Hadesburg?"

"Well, because Prince Alexander showed up, of course," said Lily. "And because several dozen other men who are looking for me are staying at the castle. I don't intend to be dragged back by any of them. I hadn't planned on running away again, though the thought did occur to me." She patted the horse on his withers. "When Prince Alexander placed the reins in my hand, it seemed too good to pass up. I did have to leave the Book of Enlightenment behind, though. If I could think of a way to get it without being caught, believe me, I would."

"No, no, no," said Marzipan, tiny hands clenching her bright blue hair. "You can't run away again. It's jus' not possible. You 'ave to go back!"

"What? Why?"

"You jus' . . . . She jus' means, you ought to have told

Persephone at least," said Beloit hastily. "Plus you could go back an' grab your book."

"That's not wot I mean at all an' you know it!" shouted Marzipan, whose wings had begun a hummingbird beat. "You 'ave ta go back, m'lady, and meet the prince again. He's de on'y one can save you from this mess you've got yourself into."

"Oh, I've made this mess, have I?" shouted Lily in turn, picking up the agitation. "I didn't set a price on my head, so that any man could kidnap me at my own father's bidding! I didn't send an evil prince like Alexander on my heels! I didn't ask for a dandy like Prince Carlton to become the front runner in the rat race for Princess Lily's tail! And if you'll recall, it was you two," she stabbed a finger in the air as she pointed at Beloit and Marzipan in turn, "who convinced me to run away in the first place!"

"I know, I know, that's not wot I meant," said Marzipan, grabbing Lily's finger with both her tiny hands. "Tisn't your fault at all. But you must trust me, and return to the castle and to Prince Alexander, right away."

"Marzipan, don't!" yelled Beloit. "You know we can't!"

"It's too late, Beloit!" Marzipan snapped back. "We can't let her go this time, or she'll be runnin' forever."

"I know, but you can't tell her! You mustn't!"

"Tell me what??" shouted Lily.

Their response was cut off by a man's voice drifting up through the trees. He must be down on the next switch-back on the hill.

"I hear voices, alright. A girl's, and two others. Maybe fairy folk. Din't ya say she had little friends? I'll bet she's up this trail, alright."

"Then by all means, follow that voice, Burly, that is if you'd not prefer to continue discussing it while the Princess escapes once more?"

Lily's eyes went black as she recognized Prince Carlton and Lord Burly's voices, and she mounted the horse as fast as she could. The fairies retreated to the saddlebags without a word and they were off like a shot. Of course, there were no guns back in the Enlightened Kingdoms, so Lily thought they were off like an arrow shot, and not a bullet like you were thinking just now, but still, an arrow shot is pretty fast.

They came over the crest of the hill, down the valley, and up the next hill. Lily chanced a look over her shoulder and to her horror, she saw more than thirty men, half of them on horseback, bearing down on her, the other half running to keep up. The riders kept to the road by necessity, but the footmen ran straight through the valley, making a B-line for her position. She kicked Milwaukee around the bend and was delighted to discover the trail forked. Without pausing to consider, she went left.

The noise of her hunters was getting louder, shouts coming around the hillside regarding her tracks and her mount. The trail she had chosen wound around a great many boulders. Suddenly around a bend it came to an end. There was no place else to go.

Lily threw herself off the horse's back and crouched behind it, looking for a place to hide. Then she heard a voice from the nearest boulder.

"Over here!"

Lily peered into the darkness. A swarthy face leaned forward into the sunlight, brown curls held back from his face. Prince Alexander held out his hand and beckoned her into the darkness.

"There's a cave. Come on. I'm your only chance for escaping from them." He beckoned again as she hesitated. "They'll be here any minute!"

She looked back toward the trail. It was impossible to tell whether they had gone the other way at the fork, and anyway there were enough of them they could easily split up. She turned back to Alexander and led Milwaukee into the recess.

There was just enough room behind the boulder for the horse to stand on level ground. She slung his reins around a rocky spike and pushed his rump out of the light. Prince Alexander grabbed a handful of rocks from the floor of the cave, then cautiously peeked out onto the trail, listening.

"No one yet." He tossed his rocks across the trail, and they rolled and bounced down the slope on the other side. A strange shriek had erupted the moment the sun had hit the stones.

"Singing crystals," he explained, turning to Lily and picking up more stones. "They sing, a little off-key, when they're in sunlight. I'm thinking if we can get enough of them out into the forest, they'll hear it and go another way."

Lily helped him pick up crystals, which covered the sloping cave floor, and throw them as far as she could down the hillside. They caused quite a din after a few handfuls, like a nest full of sick birds, quavering in a sour tone.

Sure enough, they heard men calling to each other outside the cave, and soon heading down the hill again.

Lily sat back on the sloping floor, dusting her hands and listening. The prince sat down as well, although he seemed braced, ready to spring up again at any moment.

"I think you may be alright now," said the prince after some minutes of silence. "We'll want to wait, of course, be sure they've gone. If we suspect they're coming back, we can go through the cave. I know the way." He gestured behind him, where the slope of the cave met the roof, leaving a gap the size of a barrel leading further under the hill.

Lily glanced back at the opening, then returned to looking at him with suspicion and weariness. After their gazes locked for a few moments, he said, "I know who you are."

"I suppose you'll be taking me back, for the reward?" She tried to sound casual, but it came out bitter and cold.

He laughed, without humor. "Is that what you think? That I saved you from them so that I could claim you for myself?"

She shrugged. "I would expect the same of any of them."

He shook his head, his curls springing loose from their band. "Not to sound pompous, but I don't believe I am anything like those men." He gestured at the cave's entrance. "And Beloit and Marzipan had almost convinced me you were worth all the trouble being made over you."

"Well, Beloit and Marzipan had convinced *me* that you were an evil, twisted, pig of a man who enjoys torturing little folk. So if we are both to believe them, it seems we are at an impasse."

Lily and Alexander both looked at the saddlebags, then back at one another.

"Yes, I know they're in there. What say we leave them out of it, for a bit," he said. "Clearly they aren't to be trusted."

Lily wanted to protest, but if they had been saying good things about her to Prince Alexander, it was difficult to understand their motives. She still didn't know what they had meant that Alexander was the key and why they wanted her to go back to Castle Hadesburg.

"So if you haven't come after me to claim the reward, why then? How do you come to be right here where you could save me?"

He laughed again. "Do you really think I didn't recognize you in the castle? I'll admit, the allergic reaction is quite pronounced. The disfigurement is masterful. What is it, poison ivy? Wartberry?" She turned her face away from him with a snap. "And while your description has been widely published – The Knightly Times included a portrait in the last edition – most of the people looking for you do not recall details as I do, such as your amazing eyes, which seem to change with your mood."

She snapped back around to look at him directly with those magical orbs. "So you recognized me. What of it? How came you here?"

"I followed you," he said with a shrug. "I didn't want to alarm you. I couldn't very well try to cloister you and explain myself without arousing suspicion. I must admit your fondness for retreat was almost predictable."

Lily shook her head, making waves in her long hair. The gall of this man! "Well," she huffed, "you certainly have me to yourself now. By all means, explain!"

Prince Alexander looked at her for a moment, and then sighed, turning his gaze to the cave floor. He picked up a few larger crystals and rubbed them with his thumbs, polishing off the dust. "I suppose I'm not likely to get a fair chance, no matter what I do. I may as well talk now.

"I've been courting all through the Enlightened Kingdoms for three years now. Every time I heard about a princess in whom I might be interested, I'd go to meet her, at a gala such as yours. All the princesses were so cold, so aloof. They seemed all too ready to show me I was not their type. You may not know this, but when someone doesn't like you, and you know it, it is very hard to find a way to like them. Nothing but cold shoulders everywhere I went.

"Then I met you. In the few minutes we had together, before you realized who I was, I found you charming and delicate and gracious. You even seemed to like me, if I may be bold enough to say so. After meeting you and, and chasing you, and after everything Marzi and Beloit said about you, I just, I had to know you. I wanted to understand."

"Understand what?" said Lily, tilting her head in curiosity.

"Understand who you are. Why you ran away. The other princesses, they turned away from me, they were cold and dismissive, but you were . . . fiery, you were determined, you were bloody opinionated," he shook his head at her, almost amused. "You were enchanting and intriguing one minute and screaming about the injustices of the world the next. I was utterly stunned when I found out you'd run away because of me, but thinking of how passionate you were, I didn't doubt for a minute it was your own idea. I had to know who this lovely, well-read, passionate, impetuous woman was."

He finished, staring at her with his dark brown eyes. Lily stared back, her own eyes lightening back to green. She didn't know what to make of it. He seemed so sincere. She had forgotten how good looking he was, how well spoken. He sat so close, leaning toward her now, their shoulders touching, his breath moving the trim of her bodice.

Lily shook her head to clear it, scooting away. At a

comfortable distance, she looked up at him again.

"Why did you say those horrible things when we met? If the fairies made up the stuff about torture and spying, but you really are the great man everyone says you are, why would they lie about you?"

He turned back to polishing the crystals with his thumbs. "I don't want to make you angry again by accusing them, but you really ought to learn a little more about Soula-Mays. They are a mischievous tribe. If they have played a trick on you by telling a lie, they refuse to fess up unless you ask a specific enough question to cut through their deceit. When they continue to be tricksters over a certain age, they are often sent away to learn proper behavior. Marzipan and Beloit were sent to me. Clearly I am not the teacher I thought myself.

"I suspect Marzipan and Beloit have been lying to all the women I've courted. You seem to have taken the bait more than any of them."

"And the horrible things you said to me?" asked Lily.

He shook his head a little. "I don't remember saying anything particularly horrible. I mostly remember a lovely conversation until you got upset. And I think you can forgive my saying the fairies were lying to you, with all the evidence against them."

"I haven't seen any evidence. When I mentioned Marzipan's name and said what she had told me, you called me stupid!" Lily leapt to her feet and gestured emphatically, the dramatic effect somewhat lessened by the slippery footing that caused her to totter.

"I did not call you stupid!" retorted the prince, standing up and stepping toward her. "I said Marzipan was a stupid girl, for telling such lies about her prince. Even now I don't know the reason why!"

"Well, I don't know that they are lies!" Lily shouted into his face. "Can you prove it?" When he gestured toward the horse and began to speak, she said, "And don't tell me the fairies will admit it, because for all I know, you could have threatened them again if they didn't back you up!"

He stared at her with his mouth hanging open a moment, his arms still pointing at the horse.

"I can prove it, without relying on witnesses. Milwaukee, this horse that you rode out of the Castle Starling to run away from me. He's a fine mount, yes?"

"Yes," answered Lily, not knowing what he was driving at.

"He has a particular liking for raspberry leaves, new and green as they are this time of year. You'll have seen him stop whenever he comes across them?"

"Yes," said Lily again.

"He tends to scratch at his left front leg with his teeth whenever he gets the chance. He has an old scar on the front foreleg in the shape of a crescent moon."

Lily glanced at the horse, dozing in the front of the cave, the moon-shaped scar barely visible in the fractured sunlight.

"Well, you . . . you . . ." stuttered Lily, "you could have found that out while you were riding him, after you caught the fairies." Even to her own ears it seemed a weak protest.

He shook his head a little, as if he couldn't believe she was still resisting the truth. "I suppose I could have, yes. But the reason that I know these nuances of this horse, Milwaukee – which is his real name and not just Beloit's invention – is because he is my horse. Milwaukee belongs to me."

"No!" shouted Lily in horror. "The fairies picked him out from the stables, which would mean–"

"They knew," finished the prince.

Lily stood with her mouth gaping, making little squeaking noises as she struggled to get air. It couldn't be. It wasn't possible. Milwaukee was his horse. No. Then the fairies had picked him because they knew it was his horse, sniggering as they hovered in front of the stall and whispering to each other. That meant they had wanted the prince to follow them. But why?

"Why?" Lily squeaked out finally. "Why would they want you to follow me?" She finished her thought out loud.

"I don't know," said Alexander. "Perhaps they thought you should have a second chance after the trick they'd played."

Lily tugged at her long hair, still not wanting to believe. She looked over at the saddlebags, where she could see two tiny heads of spiky hair and two pairs of eyes like sparks shining out of the darkness.

"You!" she shouted, pointing a deadly finger. "Explain yourselves!"

The twin sparks turned to look at each other, then the fairies flipped open the flap and flew out.

Marzipan was looking a bit full of herself, hovering with her arms crossed in an air of distinct pleasure.

"Ye're s'posed ta ask us specific questions," she informed them.

Lily gritted her teeth at the fairy girl, which made Marzipan lose a bit of confidence, slumping her shoulders slightly. "Why did you do this thing, tells these lies, ruin a good man's reputation, and quite possibly ruin my life?"

Beloit made a face like this was a good question, nodding in agreement at his sister.

"We was s'posed ta test the women he courted, ta make sure they were good enough," she said.

"Yeah. You passed the test wiv flyin' colors, m'lady," added Beloit brightly.

"So that business about spying, and threatening, and cutting off people's wings – that was all made up?" asked Lily.

"'Fraid so," said Marzipan with a shrug.

"And why did you steal Milwaukee?" asked Alexander, standing beside Lily and joining her interrogation. "Didn't you know I would follow?"

"A'course, we did, yer highness," said Beloit with a dismissive wave of his hand. "We counted on it. Milwaukee is yer favorite, after all."

"Indeed," he said, with a heavy breath that was the beginning of a laugh. "Why, then?"

"Well, none of de others ever wanted ta save us before,"

answered Marzipan. "She was the first ta run away. We'd on'y known her fer a few hours, but liked her immensely, right off, and when she thought she had to risk her neck to save us, we knew she was too good to pass up." She gave Lily an approving nod.

Lily answered by throwing her hands in the air and looking bewildered.

Alexander turned to her. "Do you believe me now?"

She turned to face him, standing only a few feet away. "Honestly, I don't know what to believe anymore. So many people tried to tell me how wonderful you were, and all the while I just held on to what I believed from the fairies' story. And now here you are, and here they are, and I hardly know which way is up at the moment."

He stepped forward and took her hands in his own. "Now you know I'm not the monster they said I was, at least. You could try spending time with me, get to know me, so you could make up your own mind about me. And you know," he smiled, making the princess's heart flutter, "I did come here to save you from the people chasing you."

She looked into his kindly eyes for a moment, then snapped her head to look at the fairies, realizing what he had just said.

"And that's another thing! There are really awful men out there chasing after me! And it's all your fault! How were you planning to get me out of that mess?"

Marzipan and Beloit both looked a bit sheepish, but Beloit said, "Well, the plan all along was ta get you and Prince Alexander together. And if that's happened, it'll all come out right!"

Lily turned back to Alexander, and didn't know whether to laugh, as she saw the light coming into his eyes, or to be angry again. Perhaps, if he would have her . . .

"I don't think that's something on which you ought to count, my darling," came a high sneering voice from the mouth of the cave. In all their talking, they had forgotten to listen for the return of the hunters.

Prince Carlton stood in the mouth of the cave, sword drawn, staring malevolently at the princess and her prince. He glanced sideways and saw the fairies, his evil smile falling into an ugly grimace.

"I always did detest little folk. I hope you aren't too attached to them, Princess, as I plan to have them banned from the castle," said Prince Carlton.

Lily and Alexander had frozen when they heard him speak, still holding each other's hands. Now Lily clutched at his hands as if her life depended on it.

"You may ban anything you like from your castle, Prince Carlton. It's none of my affair," she replied coolly.

He looked back at her over the point of his sword. "Oh, but it will be, my darling. It's Castle Starling I mean to take as my home."

Alexander's grip had tightened on her own at the word "darling."

"See here, Carlton," he said. "The reward decree clearly states the princess must come with the man who finds her of her own free will. It would appear to me that she doesn't want to go with you."

"Is that so, my darling?" he asked. When she shook her head, his sinister smile returned. "I can be very persuasive."

With one motion he lashed out with his free hand and scooped Marzipan into it. She screamed, as Beloit flew out of the way just in time and hovered behind Alexander. Prince Carlton got a grip on her, fist curled around her small form so that head and hands stuck out of the top. She looked miserably at her companions in constricted silence.

Holding the fairy before him, he returned to staring at Princess Lily as if she were a very nice pair of leather boots.

"What do you say, your highness? Have I got your attention? Good. Now, obviously we can't have you choosing this nancy over myself," he gave a disdainful nod at Alexander, "so I'll just have to make my own bargain. You will be coming back to Castle Starling with me, straight away. If we return to Persephone's court, she'll naturally side with her little brother. If you force me, I will hurt your little winged friends. I don't want to, darling, but you *will* continue to stand there holding hands with another man, and I am beginning to feel hurt." He cocked his head and raised his eyebrows in an attempt to look sad.

Lily and Alexander dropped hands and sprang apart.

"Please let her go," Lily said. "I'll come with you, I promise I won't fight, if you will release her unharmed."

He shook his head at her, making shameful little clucking noises. "I want to believe you, darling, but I really do need you to take me seriously."

He laid his sword tip-down in the dirt, balanced against his knee. He held his closed fist up as if to demonstrate, and with his free hand, he gently pulled one of Marzipan's skinny wrists till her whole arm stuck up from its enclosure. Even in the dim light, Lily could see tears starting to stream down Marzipan's face.

"Please!" Lily voice rose in terror. "Please, I'll do anything you want! What do you want?? Don't!!"

"Shh," said Prince Carlton softly. "You're ruining the moment. I want to enjoy this."

With the smallest of motions, his fingers and thumb squeezed together and broke Marzipan's arm. It was like the snapping of a very small twig in the echoing chamber, but the effect was that of a cannon shot. Marzipan screamed in pain.

The prince smiled. He opened his hand and blew on Marzipan as if she were an unwanted bug or grain of dust.

Several things happened all in the next moment. Alexander leapt down on Carlton, at an advantage from the slope on which he stood, and sent his shoulder into the man's chest. The sword flew out of either man's reach as they toppled to the floor, wrestling. Marzipan flew in painful loops to land in Lily's outstretched hands. Beloit threw the largest singing crystal he could hold at Prince Carlton's head, which conked him with a satisfying thud before Carlton fell under Alexander's pounce, then let out a high-pitched whine as the crystal bounced, blood-covered, into the sunlight.

Alexander yelled, "Run!" as he elbowed Carlton in the face, and took a punch to his kidney.

Lily looked out the cave mouth. There were still men out there. She held Marzipan's quivering body against her chest and motioned to Beloit, who landed on her arm to attend to his sister. Turning, she groped with her free hand up the slope of cave floor. She must get to the exit at the top of the slope, going further into the hill.

She could hear the sounds of the struggle behind her. Sudden bursts of forced breath, punches, hard slaps. Periodically Alexander cried out "Run!" again. She just had time to think of the darkness and her lack of a torch when a light caught her attention. Green lights and purple, and very bright red ones. The crystals of the cave were glowing with their own light. The exit gaped like a mouth before her, empty and pitch black. She reached out to the glowing stones. A red one the size of a grapefruit was near her free hand. She snatched it up and held it before her like a torch as she crawled on her belly into the exit.

Alexander cried, "No!" very suddenly and loudly, and she turned, fearing the evil prince had subdued him at last. But she saw he was looking up at her, staring with horror at the stone in her hand. She looked down at it and realized she couldn't feel her fingers, or her toes. A slick, cold sweat ran down her back like a snake. Her elbows felt like wings. *I was the dragon all along*, she thought. *They were my dreams.* She dropped the red crystal and fell onto her back, confusion swallowing her as she slid backwards into the dark of unconsciousness.

Part Thirteen
In which Fate is Decided

L ily rolled on her bed, twisting the silk sheets in her legs, groping for a cool spot. A voice asked if she wanted anything, and she slurped at the proffered cup of water a moment later. She rolled into a cool fold at last and fell back into unconsciousness.

She dreamed of flying, as a dragon, and then as a fairy, over the springs in the great forest. She was cold, delightfully cold as she splashed in a spring, washing her sugar glider hands and her striped face. But sitting on the rim of the pool, she grew hot in the sun, so hot, wishing she could sweat under her fur. A cool cloth patted her face and she dreamed she was at home, Martha tending her with fierce vigilance.

A man sat next to her. At first she thought it was Alexander, then she feared it was Carlton, and at last she became convinced it was her own father. Tender "there, there's" and hushing as a large hand brushed her face.

The sun was coming in the paneless window, which faced a great green expanse of lawn, with a crystal blue sky over it. Crystal. That word had meaning for our dear princess. She groped at it with her mind, trying to discover what it was. She rolled over in the large bed, not her own, nor her bedroom in Castle Starling, for that matter. Some foreign suite in an unfamiliar place. She looked at the person sitting in the chair at her bedside.

Martha looked up from the embroidery she worked, setting it in her lap. She smiled, faintly, as if not daring to hope her patient was awake. "My lady?" she asked in a hush. "You're eyes seem clearer. Are you feeling up to some broth?"

"Where . . . where am I?" whispered Lily, her voice croaking from disuse.

"Castle Hadesburg, your highness. In the guest wing. See, there's the courtyard." She pointed at the window through which the sun was streaming, and Lily could see the familiar outer wall that surrounded it. The courtyard was empty. The dragon summit must be over.

"How long . . . ?" she muttered. Martha hushed her and would answer no more questions until she had taken several spoonfuls of broth.

She had been in bed for three weeks after the incident in the cave. It was the glowing crystal that caused it. The green and purple and any colorless ones were alright, but the red ones were toxic, making her very sick. It was lucky she hadn't gone into the opening at the back of the cave, or they would have had a very bad time getting her out.

Alexander had managed to clock Carlton into unconsciousness with the butt of his sword, just after Lily fell on the near side of the ominous opening. He had bundled her and the fairies onto the horse and rode hell bent for leather back to the castle. Persephone's personal healer had seen her straight away, and they got her tucked into this nice room for visiting royalty. The healer gave her the potion for the cure, but said it could take several weeks for it to undo the damage. She had been tossing in and out of fever ever since.

Her adventures in matrimony might have been at an end, had Prince Carlton not been found in the cave shortly after Alexander left. The prince and many companions returned to the castle and accused Alexander of treachery and bodily harm, which was unfortunately in evidence on Carlton's head. They said Marzipan had been hurt in the skirmish, and demanded that they hear Carlton's rightful claim to the reward for finding Princess Lily.

As Carlton had predicted, Persephone sided with her brother. She believed Alexander's account and had said he would never have hurt his fairies. Before long, things had gotten out of hand and it had become apparent her authority was not enough to solve the problem. King William of Starling had been sent for, with a speedy dragon carrying the news. Since Lily was in no condition to be moved, the decision about what was to be done must happen in Hadesborough.

"And so we're all here, me, the King and Queen, and the princes who are bandying for your hand. His Majesty, your father, was in here until an hour ago, and then he went off to find some breakfast and get some rest," finished Martha. "And both of your princes have been to watch over you as well, one at a time. They *really* don't like each other."

"Alexander has been here?" asked Lily, sitting up against a mountain of pillows and sipping honeyed water. "Is he still in Hadesborough, then?"

"Oh yes," answered Martha with a smile. "That one's very sweet on you, comes by all times of the day and night, to sit beside you, holding your hand. He'll be very pleased you are awake at last."

"You said 'all my princes.' Do you mean Carlton, or are there more?"

"Well, more came back with him from the hills, but it seems he's enough sway to get the others to back off. Since no decision's been made over who gets to court you, he had to be allowed in to see you, same as his highness of Sweethaven." Martha wrinkled her nose and leaned in toward Lily. "I really think he only comes here for a show, to make it seem as if he's innocent. He's very awkward, doesn't know what to say to your sleeping form, or what to do with his hands."

Lily nodded slightly, the small movement seeming to take every muscle in her head and neck. She was very stiff. "He isn't innocent at all. Carlton, I mean." She stared out the window as she took another drink of water. "He hurt the fairies. Are they alright? Is Marzipan alright?" she asked with sudden fervor, feeling guilty for not asking first thing.

"Yes, she's on the mend. You'll see her soon, with her little splint and all. Fairies heal pretty quick. Couldn't live so long if they didn't, I expect."

Marzipan and Beloit were the first to visit her after she

awoke. Marzipan's arm was in a cloth sling, splinted expertly with twigs of willow. She explained that the Soula-Mays who worked at the castle had a healer who had attended her. No, it didn't hurt much anymore. She wiggled her fingers in demonstration.

Lily asked many questions about the events since her collapse. Not much more detail was available than what Martha had told her. She decided to ask about the lies the fairies had told.

"Who was it that sent you to foil Prince Alexander's courting, anyhow?" asked Lily.

"Well, we weren't exactly sent to foil it, m'lady," clarified Beloit. "Just make sure the lady was worthy, and would make up her own mind about him."

"Did you tell all the ladies the same story you told me?"

Marzipan shrugged the shoulder not wrapped in the sling. "It sorta developed over time. But somethin' similar, yeh."

"And who told you to do it?" Lily looked from one fairy to the other. "Is that not a specific enough question? Please, tell me!"

"It's on'y just, she might be mad," answered Beloit and looked away.

"It was Queen Persephone," answered Marzipan at last. "You really ought ter talk to her about it. She can explain it much better than we could."

Lily sat back on her pillows, musing. "Does Alexander know?"

Both fairies nodded. "He asked the same questions when we got back," said Marzipan. "After you was seen to, a'course."

Alexander and Persephone were her next visitors. When she saw the prince enter the room, she wanted to leap from the bed and embrace him, but propriety and her weakened state prevented it. She contented herself with reaching out her hand, which he kissed, lingering over it. He continued to hold it when he sat in the chair beside her bed.

After a few minutes of pleasant inquiries into her health, Lily spoke up. She no longer felt meek before Persephone, restored to her title as she was. True, her fate was unknown, but she was no mere Lost Girl now.

"Are you going to tell me what part you had in this game, your Majesty?"

Persephone met Lily's gaze. "I suppose the time has come for me to confess. Alexander has already heard my side of it, but you have as much right, if not more.

"Alexander believed Marzipan and Beloit came to him from their tribe, but in fact they were sent by me. During the first few years when I was married, Hal wouldn't let me come home to visit, before Mother got her way. He brought Marzi and Beloit to me as protégés. He thought they would amuse me.

"When Alexander came of age, and began to talk of taking a wife, I began to imagine how I could help him make a good match. It was around the same time that I started my halfway castle. So many girls came to me for the same reasons I had run away, because their fathers and uncles were going to make them marry someone horrible, who would beat them or isolate them or simply use them to produce an heir. The halfway castle was a way to help as many maidens as possible in my realm, but I wanted to see that Lex would not end up in an unlivable situation."

"Even though you knew I would never beat a wife or be cruel to her," interjected Alexander.

"Yes, I knew you would make a fine husband, but it was not just about the sort of man a woman marries, it's about the choices women have. I wanted your wife to choose you, to know you, to be able to judge for herself the kind of man you are and not listen to rumors or society pages or anything but her own heart when she made up her mind about you. I set about making a little test." She turned back to Lily.

"I wanted Marzipan and Beloit to be his students, to go wherever he went, and to meet the women he courted. I charged them with testing the women's characters, in any way they saw fit, so long as they caused no serious harm. They were to influence each woman and see whether she could see through it, make up her own mind about Lex and pass the test, or whether she was too easily influenced and thus not good enough for him. It was meant to give the woman a chance to make a decision about who she wanted to marry, and to see that Lex got a fiancée who was sure of herself, who would follow her own heart, as he does."

"So nevermind that you turned perfectly respectable ladies against him in the process," said Lily with disgust in her voice. "Did you intend for them to say he was maiming servants?"

Persephone shrugged, sitting back in her chair at her leisure. "The fairies had lived with me for a few years; I knew who they were, what sort of tricks they played. I didn't give specific instructions, knowing they wouldn't likely follow them anyway, but no, I certainly never intended for them to do their job so well."

"You knew who I was, didn't you?" said Lily to the queen. "That's why you spoke so much about Alexander, why you spent so much time with me."

Persephone turned her blue gaze on the princess. After a moment, she said, "Yes, I knew. Jonquilline told me." When Lily's jaw dropped, Persephone smiled. "She figured you must be someone connected with my brother because of the fairies. She'd met them here before they went to live in Sweethaven – briefly, the fairies wouldn't remember her because of all the dragons that come to the castle – and the stories you told about running away from arranged marriage made her suspicious. When we spoke just after you arrived, I helped her give you a name. Now, don't look distraught dear. The old dragon was only looking out for you. She seems quite fond."

Lily looked back at Alexander, silently holding her hand. He looked up and met her gaze.

"I am terribly sorry my family has caused all this mess," he said. "I really hope we can come through it together, you and I."

Lily smiled at him. "Between your family and mine, we've

managed to get the whole of the Enlightened Kingdoms in an uproar. I would never dream of blaming you." She reached up and stroked the side of his face. "Do you worry that Prince Carlton will win? He can't possibly have any proof to convince my father."

Alexander's eyebrows drew together in a look of concern, and he dropped his gaze to his lap. "He has managed to convince quite a few people already. The fact that I hit him over the head is hardly in my favor."

"But now I can tell people what really happened. I'll tell them about his breaking Marzi's arm. Papa will have to believe me!" Her voice rose in desperation.

He shook his head, still not looking at her. "He didn't believe you about me, when you tried to warn him. And now you've been proven wrong, and my family has shown it is capable of treachery, and of using fairies to carry out their schemes. Who knows what he will believe now?"

As it turned out, Lily only saw her father for a brief time before the day of the hearing. He came with her mother, who had been in to see Lily as she grew stronger over a period of days, walking around the guest wing and the grounds to regain her strength. She had asked to see him a number of times, and when he finally came, she understood why he had refused.

She brought up the topic of Prince Carlton and the upcoming hearing, and the king's normally jovial face fell into a flat expression.

"I won't say I told you so about fairies causing trouble, because I know you have suffered for it, sweet pea. We really cannot discuss the matter of the princes. It'll all become clear once the hearing comes," he said, patting her hand and not looking at her.

"But why not? Don't you want to know what I have to say?" she asked quietly, trying to get him to meet her eyes.

"Certainly, what you have to say is important," he said, staring over her shoulder out the window. "But yours is not the only view that matters in the . . . matter."

The Queen picked up her daughter's hand, drawing Lily's attention from her inattentive father. "What he means, dear, is that we know you have some . . . affection for the prince of Sweethaven. I'm sure anything you can tell us about what happened in that cave will be helpful, but, it's only . . . . As your parents, it is up to us to decide what is best for you. From the things being said about this prince from Sweethaven, we need to know more before we can choose him as your future husband. You understand."

The day came at last for the hearing to begin. A court with a dais had been set up in Persephone's grand courtyard, where the dragon summit had been held some weeks before. There were thrones for King William, Queen Elizabeth, Queen Persephone, and King Hal. Many seats for spectators were laid out on the grass, and a smaller, lower dais was set next to the main one for the person telling their story.

Lily was escorted to the courtyard court by the fairies and her Lost Girl friends, Aalyn, Buttercup, and Narnia. She had not seen Alexander for three days, and was beginning to wonder if he had lost interest in her. Perhaps she *wasn't* worth all this trouble. She consoled herself dimly with the idea that it would all be over soon, one way or another.

Mister Zidler, the castle concierge, stood on the dais and made a speech explaining the purpose of the hearing. He read from a scroll that contained the original offer made by the king and queen of Starling: any noble man who attended Lily's gala, who could find Princess Lily and return her to Castle Starling unharmed, would be given a week of chaperoned courting of the princess. The decision about her hand was still a matter for the king, queen, and princess to decide, but the suitor, with his $5,000 gold piece reward, would have the extra chance to convince them of his worthiness. When Lily finally and officially heard her father's bounty, she was very relieved. He had been reasonable from the start. Surely this meant he could see the truth now before him.

Prince Alexander was the first to tell his story. He emerged from a seat behind Lily where she had not seen him coming in. He walked past her to the smaller dais without looking around, but he smiled when she caught his eye as he sat down.

He told the story of meeting the princess, and chasing her to the inn and beyond, all the way to the Caves of Speelonk. He helped Lily hide from the group of hunters, so that she might choose whether to go with him. Alexander was familiar with the caves, he knew secret ways through them, having spent time there since he was a boy. He talked with Lily, explained his side, and said they were just coming to terms with each other when Carlton had interrupted them. No, he hadn't hit him on the head without provocation, he answered King William's question. No, he had not drawn his sword first. No, he answered the concierge's questions, he had not threatened Lily or the fairies or said vile things about the other prince's mother.

"And just how was it that you came to hit Prince Carlton on the head, your highness?" asked the concierge.

"He had broken Marzipan's arm, and I struggled with him as Lily got away. I had to subdue him to keep him from going after her," answered Prince Alexander in a voice of measured calmness.

"Why would Prince Carlton harm the fairies?" asked Zidler. "How would that help him win the princess?"

"He threatened her, Marzipan I mean, so that Lily would go with him back to Castle Starling for the bounty."

"But Princess Lily said she would go, did she not?" said Zidler. "So what reason would he have for carrying out his threat?"

"I don't know." Alexander shook his head. "Perhaps Prince Carlton's cruelty knows no bounds."

"I protest!" shouted Carlton from his front row seat. "He cannot be allowed to slander me openly, your Majesty!"

"Quite right, your highness," agreed King William. He turned to Alexander and said sternly, "Prince Alexander, please contain yourself to facts."

"Forgive me, your Majesty. I knew of no other way to

answer the question."

"And when you took Princess Lily into the cave, did you try anything, hmm," Mr. Zidler paused, as if trying to find a delicate way to say it, "anything . . . unseemly with the princess?"

Lily cried out in horror at this suggestion that the prince had gotten fresh with her. Persephone stifled a similar exclamation with her hand. Alexander's face grew bright red and he took a deep breath.

"I did nothing of the kind, sir," he said through gritted teeth.

"I do not make the suggestion myself, your highness, but relay only what Prince Carlton gave as the reason for your fight. You may step down, your highness."

Alexander grimaced, visibly disturbed. "If I'm not allowed to suggest Carlton's actions were cruel, I don't see why he can slander me with such lies. I never behaved in any way but the most honorable toward the princess, including that day in the cave. I only wanted to help her, and to finally explain my side of things so that she could make up her own mind. I never used a threat or evil argument, and I never laid a hand on her."

Everyone looked to King William to see how he took this speech. The king's face was impassive, plain and blank. He seemed neither impressed nor relieved. After a moment he waved a dismissive hand and said, "That will be all, Prince Alexander."

Alexander pushed himself out of the chair and strode back to his seat, so upset that he blew past Princess Lily without even looking at her.

Prince Carlton was the next to be heard. He said he had been leading the troupe of men through the hills after learning that a Lost Girl had come to the castle mere weeks before, with a rash that covered half her face. After talking to his source, he realized this was most likely the missing princess. Persephone leaned forward on her throne and asked just who his source was.

"I'm afraid I couldn't betray that person's trust, your Majesty," said the prince politely. "I wouldn't want anyone to be thrown out of the castle without any place to go just because they helped to find a royal fugitive."

Without any place to go. The phrase rang in Lily's ears, like the refrain from a terrible but catchy pop song. It had to be a Lost Girl, who each had no place to go. Caroline.

Zidler had continued with his questions while Lily hummed to herself and worked out who the source had been. Carlton said he had come upon the cave and found Lily and Alexander in a compromising position, the prince apparently manhandling the princess. Carlton drew his sword and demanded he unhand the lady. Alexander drew his own weapon and told Carlton to get out until he was finished. A struggle ensued, in which the fairy Marzipan had tried to bite Carlton's fingers, and she got thrown against the cave wall accidentally, breaking her arm. Prince Carlton had rushed to her aid and called out to the princess that she was safe now. Prince Alexander clubbed him on the back of his head, knocking him out as he bent over the poor, injured fairy.

Lily, Marzipan and Beloit all cried out this time, the princess jumping to her feet and the fairies flying over her shoulders. It took quite a lot of shushing on the part of the concierge and finally Lily's father to get them to sit down and wait their turn.

"How do you answer the allegation from Prince Alexander that you deliberately broke Marzipan's arm, your highness?" asked Zidler.

"Well, obviously he's lying," answered Prince Carlton. "He couldn't possibly admit that I had tried to help his servants, and that he had taken such despicable advantage of my philanthropic nature."

"Have you anything to prove that your version of the story is true, your highness?"

"I have my own good word, sir, and that of my companions. They saw the prince with his hands all over the princess before I entered the cave. If that much is true, then it follows that the rest of my story is correct as well."

"Yes," mumbled Zidler, looking down at a scroll, "I have the name of Lord Burly, and one Grady MacGinty, who have confirmed such a report. Each will give testimony next."

Naturally, all of Carlton's cronies confirmed his version of events.

Lily was called last. Finally, the story would be set straight, she thought.

She explained that she had taken the horse, Milwaukee, when Prince Alexander asked her to stable him, the horse. She had hidden when she heard the men coming after her. She related in detail the scene in the cave, which I'm sure you remember, and if you don't, try going back to reread the previous chapter, which will save me having to go over it all again.

"So did Prince Alexander make any ungentlemanly advances on you inside the cave, your highness?"

"No, he certainly did not," said Lily.

"But you do have affection for the prince of Sweethaven, now that you've got your stories straight?"

"I don't know about getting our stories straight. I just know now that he is not the monster I thought he was when I ran away. And as for romantic feeling," she hesitated, finding Alexander's face in the crowd. He seemed to be examining his fingernails, as if he was unconcerned about the answer, but after a moment, he lifted his head. A smile that started in his eyes and trickled down into his mouth as he looked at her made Lily tingle all over. "Yes, I'd have to say I do have affection for him."

"So if you had been doing something a maiden should not do with his highness, you wouldn't necessarily admit it here, would you?" said Zidler.

She tore her eyes away from Alexander and looked at the pompous little concierge. "I have no reason to lie, sir."

"Love is insufficient reason?" Zidler raised his eyebrows as he looked at her. "Queen Persephone, in her fervor to do right by her brother, lied to him when she sent the fairies. The fairies lied out of loyalty to their mistress and an enjoyment of mischief. Prince Alexander may have lied because he doesn't want to tarnish your name or to face such charges in this court. Yet you would not lie to be with him even though you love him? Is love not the greatest of all reasons?"

Lily looked from Zidler to Alexander, to Marzipan and Beloit, to her father and mother. "Yes, I suppose it is," she said, turning back to the concierge. "So far the only person lying here today is Prince Carlton, and he appears to love no one but himself. It would seem to me that greed is a reason used far more often for lying than is love."

It was Prince Carlton's turned to stand and sputter in protest. He didn't really have anything to say except "No!" and "She doesn't know what she's saying. Darling!" Zidler managed to settle him down, with the help of two armed comrades.

Lily stepped down and the kings and queens conferred amongst themselves. After some minutes, Queen Persephone and King Hal stood up and walked off the dais, leaving the king and queen of Starling talking together. Lily stood as Persephone approached her.

"They don't want us to help them with the decision, I'm afraid," said Persephone. "They think we are too biased towards Lex, and I must admit that I am."

"But they can't possibly believe that nonsense about us lying because we were making out," said Lily. "Even if it were true, it should show that we care for each other and that I don't care for Carlton."

Persephone shrugged. "Not if he was forcing you, it wouldn't. And if you were willing . . . . Well, it's not something parents like to picture."

Lily met her eyes and blushed a little. "It's not true anyway. Do they really seem to believe Carlton? Why didn't they call the fairies? Marzipan knows exactly who broke her arm."

"They didn't call them because they are known to be liars," said the queen. "Certainly their loyalties are mixed at best, and their lies started this trouble in the first place."

"If only there were some way to prove who was telling the truth," said Lily. "Something indisputable."

"It could save you if there were, but right now, it doesn't look good." Persephone put a sympathetic hand on Lily's shoulder for a moment, then turned away to talk to her husband.

Another hand fell on Lily's opposite shoulder, and its arm slithered around her neck. Lily turned to find Prince Carlton hugging her tight to his side, smiling an oily smile.

"Don't worry, darling. It'll all be over soon," he crooned into her ear. "Soon they'll side with me, and we'll go back to Castle Starling, and all its riches, and you'll be mine, finally, once and for all. The fairest maiden in the land will be queen to the most stylish hunter in the Enlightened Kingdoms." His lips brushed her ear as he waved his head back and forth.

Lily shivered, tried to pull away. Her mother happened to glance her way, saw the prince with his arm around her in apparent intimacy, and the queen smiled at the couple.

"Just wait. What I did to little Marzipan is nothing compared to what I'll do to you, until you admit you love me." Carlton looked into her black eyes with a heat that made the princess feel sick.

Lily spun around, out of his grasp, then slapped him soundly in the face. She stood facing him, hands clenched in impotent fury. Several nearby spectators gasped. He raised a hand to his reddening cheek, touched it gingerly with his fingers. Then a sneaking, knowing, terrible smile crinkled its way across his face. Lily didn't know what was worse, that he said nothing, or what he said with his evil smile.

"Marzipan! Beloit!" shouted the princess in desperation, turning away from Carlton and looking through the crowd for sight of the fairies. "Marzi! Where are you?"

"Here, m'lady!" came the small voice from near the front of the crowd. Marzipan sailed up, looking very sad, with her brother trailing behind her. "What is it, highness?"

"You must get into the halfway castle."

"The halfway castle? Why?" said Beloit.

"My Book is in there, and I think I know a way to prove Alexander and I are telling the truth. I never retrieved it from my room in the Lost Girls' wing after returning to the castle."

"Well, can't you just go an' get it?" said Marzipan.

"No," said Lily, looking around the crowd and lowering her voice. "They won't let me leave till the hearing's over. They're afraid I'll run away again."

Both fairies nodded.

"Even if we get the Book, how're we gonna bring it to ye? Tis much too heavy fer us ta carry," said Marzipan.

"Wait!" shouted Beloit as he clapped his hands. Then he hushed as the girls gave him duplicate stern looks for raising his voice. Surely they would think Lily and her fairy cohorts were up to something if they caused a stir.

"I've an idea," he whispered. "I know a friend who would help ye, much bigger than either o' us."

"Excellent," said Lily, "but it has to be fast. I don't know how long it will be till my parents make a decision."

"Maybe ye should try an' stall 'em," called Marzipan over her shoulder as she and Beloit flew away, putting their heads together.

Stall them. But how?

A moment later, Lily had cornered Sir Scandalot of The Knightly Times and was talking his ear off while forcefully steering him toward the dais. The short, round, balding man with a wispy grey mustache tottled along beside her.

"Now see here, princess, let go of my arm! That is no way to treat a journalist!" he said with indignation, tugging at the sleeve Lily clutched.

"Oh, but Sir Scandalot, I'm your biggest fan! And I was just thinking how wonderful it is of you to come here *personally* to write about my little story! It's just so *amazing* to have you here in person, the famous writer!" Her voice rose flirtatiously as she propelled him forward.

The old man grinned under his whiskers. "Well, my dear, you are the biggest story in the Enlightened Kingdoms just now. I look forward to interviewing you and your parents after the hearing."

"Oh *no*, Sir, think how lack-luster it would be to tell what had happened after the fact. It's so boring, so black and white. You need to be in the fray, in the thick of it. Imagine how *fantastic* a story it could be if you gave a play-by-play of the decision from right in the middle of it!"

She hauled the journalist, who was now smiling faintly and nodding his head in an agreeable sort of way, in front of the thrones. The king and queen stopped speaking abruptly and looked at her.

"Lily!" scolded the queen. "You cannot be up here while we make our decision! Go away at once."

Lily completely ignored her mother. "Your Majesties, I would like to introduce a man who is famous beyond words, more famous than me even, who has helped my story become the thing of legend that it is now. This," she let go the old man's arm and held out both hands at him in grand presentation, "is Sir Scandalot, of The Knightly Times!"

"Pleasure to meet you at last, your Majesties," said Sir Scandalot with a bow.

"Yes, and to meet you," said the king. "Now, Lily, this is no time for introductions. You must leave your mother and I alone just now."

"But Papa, just think what this man has done for us. Your bounty would never have reached so many men if he hadn't written about it. You should be grateful," said Lily.

"Actually, the princess gave me a wonderful idea for the piece I'm writing on today's proceedings. Would it be acceptable to your Majesties if I listened in while you make the decision? I'm certain my readers would get an incredible thrill out of feeling like they were here, in the moment." He smiled charmingly at them in turn.

"Certainly not," said the queen. "I'm sure you are a perfectly fine journalist, but now is not the time. And as for you," she pointed at her daughter, "I don't know what you are up to, but you can't interrupt us like this. Go back to your seat and prepare to receive our decision."

Lily went cold and her eyes darkened. She swallowed, and finally said, so quietly it was scarcely more than a whisper, "You mean, you've already decided?"

"Yes. Now, go sit down."

Suddenly there was a commotion in the crowd. People were looking up at the side of the castle wall that faced the courtyard. "What is it?" asked one onlooker.

"Why – I think it's Maltese," said Persephone, shielding her eyes with one hand as she looked up at the castle. "What can she be doing at a window of the Lost Girls' wing?"

Lily, her father and mother, and Sir Scandalot turned and looked up. Four floors up, she saw a large red dragon flying in front of one of the windows. The dragon flew away from the wall, clutching something in her hands. She circled around the courtyard, descending. Then a large square of cloth flew out of the same window, flapping in the spring breeze. It seemed to have direction, flying down to the spot behind the audience where the red dragon had landed, and Lily saw the corners were held by Marzipan and Beloit.

"I 'ave it, yer majesties, yer 'ighnesses!" said the dragon, approaching the audience from the back. "I 'ave the answer, the thing that'll prove Princess Lily is telling the truth!" Lily thought the voice sounded familiar.

The dragon stopped when she reached the back of the audience. She could not fit down the aisle without toppling several people on either side of the aisle with her enormous wings.

The fairies landed on the ground in front of the dragon, covering her with the bed sheet. The dragon's head appeared over the sheet for a moment and then was gone in a flash of light, blurring at the edges. The dragon disappeared and the sheet descended, covering a person-sized shape, which turned around and wound itself in the fabric. Lily was surprised to see (and I expect you will be, too) that the person standing there in a makeshift toga was none other than Heddy Winchester.

"I 'ave it!" she proclaimed again, waving Lily's Book of

Enlightenment in her hand. "Ye'll 'ave ta pardon me dress, sires. I'm not fitted out for such an occasion as this, but I'd never make it to the stage in me dragon form. And if I'd turned human with nuthin' on, you'd be in for quite a sight o' me naked, so take me as I is." She muttered her way up the aisle and onto the dais. Lily stepped out of her way, trying to hide her grin. Heddy presented the Book to Queen Elizabeth with a little flourish.

The queen took the Book on her open hands and let Heddy flip to the index.

"Caves of Speelonk, happenings four weeks hence," she commanded.

The Book's pages fluttered.

The king and queen leaned in to read from it. Lily peeked anxiously over her father's shoulder.

The queen sat back with a smile on her face. "This is Lily's Book of Enlightenment," she explained to the crowd. Several people in the audience twittered, wondering what this meant.

The king stood up with the Book in his hands. "It seems we were about to make a terrible mistake. If I'm reading this correctly, then my daughter was telling the truth, and Prince Carlton was lying." He read from the Book.

> *In the Caves of Speelonk, Princess Lily of Starling hid from Prince Carlton of East Cloudland and his comrades. She hid with two despicable fairies from Ma-Soula, who had entrapped the fanciful princess with their schemes and ridiculous stories. In the cave she met Prince Alexander of Sweethaven, the owner of the nefarious fairies, who tried to get her to see through their veil of lies. Just as they were realizing the truth about each other, Prince Carlton caught them. He threatened one of the Little People to make Lily come with him. Even though she agreed, Prince Carlton broke the fairy's arm anyway, just to make his point. Lily was poisoned by a toxic rock, and Prince Alexander helped her get away by subduing the other prince. P.S. Even with broken arms I don't like fairies.*

Many people in the audience muttered approval at this, while certain others twittered a little.

"Why does that book hate fairies so much?" asked someone in the crowd.

"The Book of Enlightenment is different for every reader," answered Lily, stepping forward. "Its magic taps into the collective unconscious, getting its information from the wisdom of the universe. The content is always the same, but the words are particular to whomever is reading it."

She took the Book, with permission, from the king, and read.

> *Prince Alexander was eager to meet Lily again and see if she lived up to his dreams of a woman who was worldly, charming, passionate, and kind. The patient, handsome, literary prince wanted to explain the well-meant trick her fairy companions had played, hoping to help him find a good mate. He gave her the chance to choose whether to go with him, showing his heart to be as kind as his soft brown eyes, but they were interrupted by the cruel and greedy Prince Carlton. He threatened prince and princess, breaking the arm of the fairy Marzipan.*

"The text is different for me, you see," she said to her father who looked over her shoulder. "Anyone here can look at it and see the truth. Although Prince Carlton's version will likely have some differences of interpretation, the facts remain the same."

All eyes turned to Prince Carlton, standing at the front of the crowd. Without a word, he strode forward and seized the Book from Lily's hands. The people on the grass could not see what was going on, but Lily knew the Book was changing as Carlton held it. Her parents leaned over his shoulders, one on each side, to read what the Book said in his hands. Sir Scandalot managed to get a peek as well.

Queen Elizabeth gasped, and blushed, and covered her mouth.

King William cried out, "Good goblins!"

Sir Scandalot's eyebrows rose and he shot a disgusted look at Prince Carlton.

Prince Carlton glanced around at the queen and king, dropped the Book as if it were a hot root vegetable, and fled.

The crowd cheered and roared. "Princess Lily is saved!"

Lily hugged her parents in turn, then decided to hug Sir Scandalot. People came up to the dais to congratulate her, shaking her hand and patting her on the back. Before long she was making her way through the audience to greet all her well-wishers and Lost Girl friends.

The activity swirled around her, people talking and moving, congratulating each other now. She saw what looked like a few bets being paid off. Lily felt a hand clasp her own from behind and be lifted as someone kissed the back of it. She turned, preparing for another congratulations.

Alexander kissed her, quickly, feverishly, as if he couldn't help himself. He pulled back to look into her eyes and said in a rush, "I'm sorry I've stayed away from you, that I kept you at arm's length these past few days. I was so afraid of losing you that I couldn't bear to be close. I knew the more I saw you, the more I would fall –"

Lily stopped his apology by kissing him full on the mouth, holding his hand in one of her own. Alexander held the back of her head and they melted into the embrace. The world got quiet. The din of the crowd muted, and Lily's fear drained out through her feet. The kiss washed her in a warm glow. It was as if they were the only two people standing in the courtyard, in the castle, in the universe.

Part Fourteen
In which Lily Makes Up Her Own Mind

T here was much backing and forthing about where, exactly, the wedding should take place. Castle Starling was an obvious choice, but so was Castle Sweethaven, and Persephone even proposed they hold it at Castle Hadesburg because it was a neutral location. King Kazeus of Sweethaven wouldn't hear of it, having already lost one child to a wedding in that place. Persephone and Alexander's mother, Queen Demi, reminded Persephone it was time for her yearly visit home for the summer, so they could all go back to Sweethaven together but this failed to settle the argument.

As the debate waged in the throne room, Princess Lily ran up the stairs to the halfway castle wing. She nearly collided with Aaron who was standing still at the top of the stairs.

"Hello," said Lily, making him start and turn quickly around. Seeing who it was, he smiled and his shoulders collapsed in relief.

"Hello, Perviolet," he said.

"Have you by chance seen Prince Alexander? I've been looking for him."

Aaron shrugged. "Not since breakfast."

He seemed to be at a loss. "What are you doing in the halfway castle wing?" she asked. They started down the hall toward reception.

"I was looking for, um." He shook his head. "There are these Lost Girls who live here, you know. Persephone keeps them until they can find homes or husbands and, um." He trailed off.

Lily couldn't help smirking. "Have you come courting, Aaron? Perhaps that's why you and Jonny haven't left yet?"

A slow grin widened his mouth and he hung his head forward so his blond hair flopped in front of his sheepish face.

"Yeah."

"Well, good for you! Don't just stand there, tell me who she is. I know all the Lost Girls in residence. Maybe I can help you."

He brightened at this, standing up straight, his hair flopping out of his face once more. "It's the beautiful, lovely, magnificent maiden, Caroline."

"Oh," said Lily, in consternation. "And does she like you?" She tried her best to sound kind and encouraging.

"Oh yes." He nodded. "Since we met during the summit, she's been reading everything she can about green dragons, and patrols and body-guarding. And," he held up a triumphant index finger, reminding Lily of the way he brandished his sword, "hornyculture. That's the studies of plants, so she can grow the best strawberries in the land."

Lily looked away from Aaron's eager gaze. "I don't know, Aaron. She's not the nicest girl you could've picked. You really ought to know more about a person before you think of marriage."

"But Caroline *is* nice!" said Aaron, agitated. "She's not who you think, Perviolet, honestly. You must tell the queen I'm a good match, or I'll never be able to marry her." He grabbed Lily's hand and clasped it to his chest, saying "please," over and over again.

The door to the private chambers opened and Caroline stepped into the hall. Lily immediately dropped Aaron's hand and took a step backwards, inwardly bracing for a lash from Caroline's jealous tongue.

"Hello, your highness," said Caroline to Lily in apparent sweetness. "I'm so glad the book helped at your hearing," said Caroline. "When the fairies told me to get it from your room, I thought it was finally my chance to show there was no hard feelings, about the prince."

Lily nodded, staring at the girl. "Does it also make up for telling Carlton who I was?"

Caroline's brown eyes grew wide. "My lady, your

highness, I . . . I said no such thing!" she sputtered.

Lily tilted her head in disbelief. "And just who else was there to inform him? You hated me from the moment I set foot in this castle."

Caroline looked truly distraught, almost on the verge of tears. "I . . . I'll admit I was a little distant when you arrived, but really it was only because I was so saddened thinking about Prince Alexander. I never hated you. I heard a rumor that it was one of the gatekeepers who told them. One fellow saw you leave with the dark horse that day you went into the hills."

Lily was surprised to hear this, but after a moment, she realized it made sense. They had known exactly where to look for her, so the guard must have seen which direction she had gone. She shook her head a little; he'd seemed so nice. *Just because someone seems charming . . . .*

She smiled and shook Caroline's hand, glad to have been wrong about her. She thanked her for delivering the Book.

"Aaron, I'll be speaking to Queen Persephone this afternoon." Perhaps it was best for both of them if Caroline took Aaron as the model from which she drew herself.

The blond knight smiled, blushed. He looked at Caroline, then back to Lily, and nodded.

"Good day, your highness." Caroline curtseyed to Lily and turned to Aaron. "You're just on time, Aaron. Where is it we're going today?"

Aaron stuck out his elbow for her to take and led lead her down the hall. "Well, I've decided it's time for you to meet the great and wonderful Jonquilline. She's really the only family I have, aside from my brothers and sisters of course, and my parents. . . ." His voice trailed off as they reached the stairs and Lily couldn't help watching as Caroline, sour and lonely no more, seemed to soak up his every word.

Lily searched the common rooms of the Lost Girls' wing, as Alex sometimes talked to them and helped them learn to read, but he wasn't there.

She was just crossing the entrance hall toward the library

when Marzipan and Beloit appeared.

"M'lady!" Marzipan practically screamed, as she launched like a bee for the princess's face.

"Thank you!" The fairy kissed her all over her cheeks and forehead. "Thank you! Thank you! It's the most wonderful present I could have asked for!"

"They've arrived, then? That was quick."

"Pendrill and Danny brought them. All the dresses in this year's fashions. I know those guys from my Soula-May village. They said you'd asked them to come and bring the dresses and I get to pick whatever I want for the wedding!"

Lily thought all the trouble Marzipan had caused was almost worth it when she saw genuine delight in her purple eyes.

Almost.

"And they told us about the menu!" said Beloit. "Authentic Soula-May sautéed chickadee and Silver-Grape Wine. I can hardly wait for the wedding, m'lady."

A queer shadow passed over Lily's face. "Yes, right. Have you seen Alexander? I really need to speak to him."

"He's in the library. We just left him," said Beloit.

"Is everything alright, m'lady?" asked Marzipan.

She shook her head and smiled an unconvincing smile. "I'm sure it will be. See you later."

As she entered the library, the princess saw his dark curls over the back of the little settee, which Persephone had called a loveseat. He was alone, in the tall room with high shelves and tall windows to let in good reading light. As she came around the loveseat, his face was warm in the afternoon sun, and she felt a happy ping in her belly just to see him.

He smiled at her as he looked up from his book. "Any decision yet?"

Lily knew he meant the location of their wedding. "No, they're still deep in argument." She sat down beside him. "But I wanted to talk to you."

"Oh dear," he said, putting aside his book and giving her his full attention.

"I have a proposal for you," she said.

"Didn't we already do that part?"

"Yes, well. I suppose, then, what I have is . . . an unproposal?"

Before the shock could march all the way across his face, she blustered on. "I don't mean we would never have our wedding, but there's so much I want to do. Wouldn't it be nicer if we could travel together for awhile? We could see the Soula-May village, when Marzi and Beloit are ready to go back. Perhaps we could visit other fairy tribes, too. . . ."

"I don't understand. Do you . . . not want to marry me? Do you not want me as your husband?"

She scooted closer to him, put her legs in his lap. She was eager to keep the hurt from advancing in his eyes. "No, that's not it. I do want to be with you. I just wish we could be married without a wedding. All those people looking at us, expecting us to smile and dance for them, like our love is a play they get to watch. After all the scandal and sensation, I don't want to be in the spotlight for awhile. It feels like we lost so much time together already, just being ourselves."

He chuckled. "We've been together every day since we were betrothed."

"But all those days before, after we met and I was on the run. I wish I could go back to all the places I went so I could replace the evil thoughts I had about you with good ones. I want to take you with me, quietly, not in a royal caravan with an enormous wedding entourage."

"So, it's not marrying me that's bothering you. It's the wedding?"

"Precisely."

Alexander sighed. Lily noted the pleasant sensation of lift and fall of his big chest.

"You realize that while you've been unproposing to me, you've climbed into my lap?"

It was true. They were alone in the library, so rare in a castle with so many attendants. A proper princess hardly ever allows others into her personal space, but Lily's boundaries had dissolved with Alexander. Her legs had gone in his lap and then his arm naturally went around her back, and before she knew it she was sitting sideways on him with their arms around each other, faces inches apart.

Lily lay her head on Alexander's broad shoulder. "What shall we do?"

"I think I know of a way. Do you trust me?"

She sat up and looked into his brown eyes with her own clear green ones. "I do."

They went to the throne room, where their royal parents still argued over wedding sites. The kings and queens were looking frustrated as they tried to think of points for their side that hadn't already been said.

The room fell silent as the princess and prince marched in to the center and stood before the thrones.

"Beg pardon for the intrusion, your majesties," said Alexander, "but her highness and I have a request."

King Kazeus waved away his son's apology. "We weren't getting anywhere anyway. What is it?"

"According to ancient tradition in Sweethaven, a couple may be united using the ceremony of handfasting. With their promise of love and faithfulness, their hands are bound by a cord, and their bond sealed. If either person wishes to end the union, all they have to do is declare it in the first hundred days."

Queen Demi and King Kazeus were nodding, familiar with the ritual. Queen Elizabeth and King William looked puzzled, and Lily turned to Alexander.

"So it's like a temporary marriage?"

"It's a real marriage. If it isn't broken, it becomes permanent on day 101."

Princess Lily's mind turned it over, looking at this shiny thing from different sides.

"And it is a simple ceremony that can be done anywhere, without audiences or feasts or fancy dress. A promise of love between two people," said Alexander, looking into her eyes.

"Simple as that."

That was all it took for her to see his plan.

"We wish to be handfasted," said the princess to the queens and kings. "Today. Right now, in fact."

The queens and kings blew and sputtered a bit, surprised by this sudden turn. "What about the wedding plans?" asked King William. "What about where we will hold it, and inviting everyone?"

Alexander spread his hands. "You'll have a hundred days to make the arrangements and send out the invitations. Her highness and I will be handfast today and on day 100, we'll hold the royal wedding. In the meantime, we plan on travelling the countryside, discreetly, with only Martha, the fairies and a footman or two, and touring our kingdoms."

"That's plenty of time to get everything ready," Princess Lily chimed in. "Since you've already agreed on our union, there should be no objection to doing it now instead of waiting."

The fairies, who had entered the throne room with Martha and Persephone, untied a golden rope from one of the golden curtains. They flew it over to the couple.

"Will this do?" asked Marzipan.

Persephone stepped forward, catching the flying rope. She looked at her brother and her protégé in turn. "You're sure you're not rushing into this?"

Prince Alexander smiled at his bride. "Not a moment too soon."

Princess Lily smiled back. "No. I've made up my own mind."

A certain amount of muttering between the parents seemed required, but before long, they gave their consent.

Lily and Alexander held hands, and Persephone began knotting and wrapping the golden cord around them. Each in turn said the words of the ancient vow.

> *I promise to be your partner, your friend, and your true love. I promise to tell you the truth and to believe in you.*

I promise to protect you, to care for you, in easy times and hard, for all my days to come.

Everything else faded away, as if they were the only two people in the room, alone in the world together, existing only where their hands clasped and their eyes met. As they spoke the words of bond to each other, the vows they made in their eyes and in their hearts were the ones they would keep, through mischief and machinations, bad press and good gossip, till they lived happily ever after.

For at least ninety-nine of those first hundred days, anyway.

The End

Acknowledgements

Thank you to my writer's group, who saw every draft of this fairy tale and encouraged me even as they red-inked it: Justin Barba, Bob Lovely, Kendra Lisum, Julia Ballas. Thanks to Debbie Spurlock, my inimitable mentor in all things personal and professional. Thanks to Holly Frydenlund for being the best best friend a girl could have, and supporting not just my writing, but my multifarious dreams and schemes. Thanks to all the friends, too many to name, who read this book and told me they loved it and not to give up.

Thanks to my mother, Marcia Lauzon, for telling me I was a writer from such a young age that I grew up believing I already was one. Thanks to my father, Edward Schalk, for always telling me I could do anything. Thanks to Oz and Moya for putting up with Mommy's shenanigans.

Thanks to the team at 100Covers for the amazing job on my cover. They'll do one for your book at www.100covers.com. Amazon and IngramSpark were also easy to work with to get this baby published.

Thanks most of all to my husband, Josh Aronoff, for always betting on me. Here's to the long haul.

All the best,
Ella Arrow

About the Author

Ella Arrow believes in magic, especially the kind we make for ourselves. Alter ego of Elizabeth Aronoff, she writes fairy tales, urban fantasy, steampunk, horror, and many short stories based on weird ideas that blindside her in elevators and on long walks through creepy woods. You can find her at www.ella-arrow.com; on Facebook and Twitter; or in a Victorian house in a small town outside Madison, Wisconsin, chasing her kids and her next novel idea.

Made in the USA
Monee, IL
06 November 2019